I0761985

not like before

(an ilse beck fbi suspense thriller—book 6)

ava strong

Ava Strong

Bestselling author Ava Strong is author of the REMI LAURENT mystery series, comprising six books (and counting); of the ILSE BECK mystery series, comprising seven books (and counting); of the STELLA FALL psychological suspense thriller series, comprising six books (and counting); and of the DAKOTA STEELE FBI suspense thriller series, comprising three books (and counting).

An avid reader and lifelong fan of the mystery and thriller genres, Ava loves to hear from you, so please feel free to visit www.avastrongauthor.com to learn more and stay in touch.

ISBN: 978-1-0943-9487-9

BOOKS BY AVA STRONG

REMI LAURENT FBI SUSPENSE THRILLER

THE DEATH CODE (Book #1)
THE MURDER CODE (Book #2)
THE MALICE CODE (Book #3)
THE VENGEANCE CODE (Book #4)
THE DECEPTION CODE (Book #5)
THE SEDUCTION CODE (Book #6)

ILSE BECK FBI SUSPENSE THRILLER

NOT LIKE US (Book #1)
NOT LIKE HE SEEMED (Book #2)
NOT LIKE YESTERDAY (Book #3)
NOT LIKE THIS (Book #4)
NOT LIKE SHE THOUGHT (Book #5)
NOT LIKE BEFORE (Book #6)
NOT LIKE NORMAL (Book #7)

STELLA FALL PSYCHOLOGICAL SUSPENSE THRILLER

HIS OTHER WIFE (Book #1)
HIS OTHER LIE (Book #2)
HIS OTHER SECRET (Book #3)
HIS OTHER MISTRESS (Book #4)
HIS OTHER LIFE (Book #5)
HIS OTHER TRUTH (Book #6)

DAKOTA STEELE FBI SUSPENSE THRILLER

WITHOUT MERCY (Book #1)
WITHOUT REMORSE (Book #2)
WITHOUT A PAST (Book #3)

PROLOGUE

Samuel Jerome moved through the metal forest at night, one leg dragging slower than the other. His flashlight swished as he grunted and, wincing, rubbed at his bad leg. “Damn cold,” he muttered to himself, his breath fogging the chilly air.

He limped along the dusty, dirt strewn pathway meandering through the scrapyard. Occasionally he'd hear a soft *clink* of metal as he kicked a washer or a discarded screw. Every time this happened, he grumbled beneath his breath. The younger workers didn't take the job seriously enough.

His flashlight beam illuminated old, rusted vehicles lined along the side of the path. Some of them had weeds coming out the windows where the overgrowth had been left unattended for too long. There were refrigerators and old microwaves, with the parts stripped. A few shipping containers contained all manner of old bed springs and box screws. The place had a bit of a personality. The scrapyard always felt peaceful at night. No sounds here. The closest highway was too far to hear anything. But above, against the clouds, he occasionally caught the flash of headlights as the vehicles zipped by in the distance.

His own beam of light moved along the row of cars.

He went still.

He frowned, aiming the flashlight.

No weeds around the base of this automobile. A new arrival?

He didn't recognize it. Generally he was around when they received vehicles, as he liked putting old cars back together in his spare time, and would occasionally barter the boss for parts.

This Buick, though, was facing the wrong direction. It still had its tires. No overgrowth. And it wasn't facing the road like the others.

He scowled, slowly, hesitantly moving towards the car. He wasn't sure what made him pause. But a sixth sense caused him to go still on the old, grease-stained junkyard road.

He flashed his light towards the front seat.

It had been difficult to see from the path, but now that he'd gotten closer, he thought he spotted a figure sitting on the driver's side.

His heart pounded. His temper followed. "You can't be in here!" he called, his voice shaking.

No response. He circled, taking a couple of steps to the side, still aiming his light. "*Hey*, you in there!"

There was definitely a driver. The figure didn't look back. Didn't move, didn't blink.

By now, Samuel was growing uncomfortable. This wasn't the sort of thing they paid him for. He'd chased off more than his fair share of kids in the past but usually a good shout or the sound of a few of the dogs was enough to get them running.

But this fellow sat motionless. Indifferent.

Fear and frustration competed for dominance. With a shaking hand, still limping slowly forward, he pulled his phone from his pocket. No sense in playing the hero, much better to call for backup.

"I'm calling the police!" he shouted.

The man in the car didn't move. And only then did it strike Samuel that perhaps the trespasser needed help.

"Are you all right?"

Even as he said it, he spotted the blood trickling down the side of the man's head. Also streaked along his tensed knuckles gripping the steering wheel.

Now, Samuel Jerome's heart leapt. He took a couple more hurried steps towards the car, his feet scraping against the ground.

His light shone through the window now that he'd completely circled to the side. As he stared into the car, his eyes widened in horror.

A young man was sitting in the driver's seat. His eyes were closed. Blood stained the side of his face and his hands around the steering wheel.

"Hey, you in there. Are you okay?"

Samuel cursed, pounding on the glass. The young man didn't respond. The old junkyard employee's hand darted towards the handle. He tried to pull it. It wouldn't budge.

He hissed, glancing at the metal door, and then realized that someone had welded the door to the frame of the car. The metal was bubbled and warped and meshed together.

His heart was pounding wildly. The pain in his leg intensified. He cursed, flipping his flashlight, aiming, turning away so no glass would get in his eyes, and slamming the metal base into the back window.

Glass shattered. He let out a breath, tenderly guiding his arm through the window towards the lock of the front door.

"I'm calling for help!" he said. "Young man, can you hear me?"

A second later, he realized how stupid it was to try the door from the inside. It was welded. It wasn't moving, even unlocked.

Samuel tentatively reached towards the front seat, chills along his arms, down his spine. His fingers touched the young man's shoulder.

Cold as ice. Trembling, he reached up, looking for a pulse. None to be found.

The man was dead. And yet his hands gripped the steering wheel.

Now, with a sudden, daunting sense of fear, Samuel spotted the wire wrapped around the man's wrists, holding them against the wheel.

"What in the world..." he murmured.

And then he spotted the spike. Straight through the back of the headrest. It looked like it probably went far enough to pierce the head, holding it upright.

The man was dead. Someone had posed him as if he were driving the car.

Samuel Jerome screamed, stumbling away from the car and hitting the dirt road. He shuffled back, wincing and grabbing at his leg.

Under the watch of night, alone in the junkyard, crawling on the dirt away from a dead man, he fished out his phone. Dropped it.

Picked it up again. Damn it. The screen was cracked.

He lifted the device, and, desperately, dialed 911.

CHAPTER ONE

Ilse scowled in frustration and let out a sigh, causing an errant fringe from her dark hair to lift then flutter back as she listened to the music playing from her dumb phone.

Sitting at her kitchen table, her dinosaur of an old desktop computer whistled and whined as she stretched its processing power to full capacity. Green text scrolled across her screen, and she leaned in, reading the names slowly and taking mental notes.

Briefly, the generic hum of guitar and piano ceased emitting from her flip-phone. She shot a look of anticipation towards the thing, but then scowled as the holding music started from the beginning.

Dr. Beck sighed, leaning back in her chair and glancing at the clock above her table. Nearly 9:21. She'd been on hold for almost a half-hour. Time mattered to Ilse—promptness mattered. The German prison official on the other line had insisted it would only take a few minutes to get the information Ilse wanted.

Those minutes had just sped past the half-hour mark, waving where it disappeared into the rearview mirror. But Ilse was patient. She tapped her foot nervously against the floor, returning her attention to her computer screen.

On one hand, she was waiting to hear back from her father's prison. But while she waited, she scanned patient files from the last decade. Her own patients.

She tapped a finger against the screen beneath an unfamiliar name. "How about you?" she murmured. She clicked on the file, and it took her a moment to navigate the device. Computers, technology, none of it had ever much appealed to her. She didn't even have a normal stove—just a wood burning oven.

Her phone couldn't connect to the internet, or GPS, nor could it *tweet.* She preferred it that way.

As she read the file of the patient in question, her brow furrowed. The profile didn't match. She clicked back to the main registration page.

Hundreds of clients had seen her over the years. It was like looking for a needle in a haystack—and yet that was the task before her.

She needed to find that needle.

The little prick that had sent her postcards over the last few months. Taunting, teasing, mocking cards. Most likely anti-social personality disorder. She trusted her notes to narrow down whether any of her own patients had been behind the cards.

But so far, no luck.

She scrolled down the list, her eyes strained from staring at a screen for so long.

And then the music coming from her phone went quiet again.

She perked up, staring at the device. The music didn't continue.

"H—hello?" she asked.

"Yes," the voice on the other end said, the German accent all too apparent. "This is Warden Schuler. Who am I speaking to?"

"Agent, er, Dr. Beck," she said quickly. In this situation, Ilse wasn't certain which credential might open the door faster. And where her father was concerned, speed was key. She'd learned this the hard way for most of her childhood, tormented, along with her siblings, by the man in that horrible basement.

Knowing he was in prison, surrounded by concrete, just like he'd kept his kids, had given her some sort of solace... But now? She could feel her pulse quickening. How *dare* they try and release him?

"Yes, well, er, Agent-doctor," the warden said in that uptight, stiff way long-term bureaucrats mastered. "The information you request will take a few days."

"Wait, why? I'm just looking for the date of his parole hearing."

"Yes, but the prisoner in question is maximum security. Prison protocol is to go through BKA when external agencies request information."

"I—I don't understand. I just want to be at the hearing."

"It will only be a few days, I'm sure," said the warden in a very bored tone.

Ilse resisted the urge to slap her desk. She bit her lip, considering her options, then said, quickly, "Would it matter if I was the prisoner's daughter?"

A pause. A faint exhale. "You are related to Gerald Mueller?"

"Yes," Ilse said insistently.

"You wish to testify on his behalf at the parole?"

Ilse's nose wrinkled. She angrily brushed her hair past her scarred ear. "No!" she snapped. "I aim to testify *against* his release. I'm asking as a daughter. Not as an agent."

The warden sighed.

"Please!" Ilse insisted. "Surely there isn't a policy against telling a daughter when her father's parole hearing is."

Another long, world-weary sigh. "We have on record that Gerald has children. Did you visit the prison recently?"

"Yes, yes I did!" Ilse said suddenly. The visit hadn't been a social call, but she decided not to add this part.

"In that case, no information may be shared with foreign governments pertaining to the location of maximum-security prisoners," he said, somehow making every word dull and gray with his tone. "Understood?"

"Understood!" Ilse said, trying to keep the eagerness from her voice.

"Next week. Tuesday. Noon. Family or representation only!" he said.

"Got it. Thank you!"

He hung up.

The droning, holding music mercifully ceased, and Ilse slowly pocketed her phone. She frowned at the computer screen displaying the names of her patients from over the years.

Her father wasn't the one taunting her. That much was clear now. He couldn't have been the one sending the postcards. Someone on his behalf?

It didn't really matter if he was involved or not.

He couldn't be let out of prison.

They didn't know him like she did. Ilse was determined to do everything in her power not only to show up at that parole hearing, as horrible as it would be to share a room with father, but also to make sure they kept him locked away indefinitely.

It was the only way to keep others safe.

To keep herself safe.

As she considered this, she was jarred from her thoughts as her phone began to buzz. She stared, blinking—but not the warden this time. She leaned in, staring at the number, and winced. Shit. The boss was calling.

CHAPTER TWO

Agent Tom Sawyer sat in his truck, his hooded eyes fixed on the gray building beyond the chained fence. The faint odor of sandalwood and sawdust lingered in his borrowed vehicle. The license plate wouldn't check out if anyone ran it. The windows were slightly tinted, hiding him from the cameras. For now, he was here on a fact-finding mission.

He watched as the guards changed and checked his watch. His finger tapped against the glass face of the device.

"Bingo," he muttered to himself.

Now would be the perfect point for entry. He wasn't going to breach the place guns blazing, of course. But the more confusion, the better. He already had a fake ID and a badge lined up. He already knew his entrance strategy. He'd been tracking the shifts and guard changes. A couple of the guys at this facility would even recognize him. But he knew when they were off and was planning to strike when no one would know who he was.

No one except for that psycho in solitary.

Agent Tom Sawyer's fingers tensed against his steering wheel, and his eyes narrowed as he stared beneath his baseball cap towards the prison.

The monster had killed his sister. Had played with Sawyer. Had intended to cause Tom suffering.

He could still remember his baby sister, her smile, her laugh. She had been one of his best friends. Hell, one of his only friends.

And that monster inside those gray walls had taken her from him.

It seemed only right that Sawyer return the favor.

As he sat there, inhaling the recycled ventilation, he could feel his temper rising. Why did that man deserved to breathe for another second when his sister was in the ground?

It wasn't fair.

His teeth pressed tightly together, and he inhaled shakily, trying to think straight. Part of him wanted to go there now. Wanted to just march through those gates, use his own ID, and get a shot at the prisoner that way.

But no. No, he wouldn't give that monster the satisfaction of taking out *two* Sawyers. Tom still had to figure out an exit strategy.

He rubbed his chin, his fingers testing the bristle. Beyond all of that, he knew there was another problem.

Dr. Beck. Ilse had a way of prying into people's business. She didn't really mean to. It was almost as if she couldn't help herself. She was inquisitive by nature. Clever. Good at her job. Both jobs.

Tom admired her. But having her snoop around would only make things more difficult.

No, he would have to figure this one out on the down-low, without letting Beck sniff out his intentions. She'd asked questions the last time they'd been on a case together. Prying questions. Almost as if she thought she could help him. Trauma counseling.

He snorted, adjusting the brim of his baseball cap to block out the sun.

He didn't need counseling. He needed a couple of minutes alone with the monster, and a body bag. And maybe a spare shovel.

His fingers drummed against his leg, and he reached to turn the key.

Just then, his phone began to ring.

Tom wasn't one to show his emotions. Inwardly, he jolted with fear. Was that the alarm? A second later, his mind registered the device on the seat next to him. Outwardly, he didn't so much as twitch. He glanced slowly over at the phone.

The supervising agent was calling. He'd once punched the man. This wasn't a social call. Work.

He sighed, reaching out and picking up the phone. He didn't even wait for the voice to say anything.

"Case?" Sawyer guessed. Again, he didn't wait for a response. "On my way."

He hung up before Rawley could get a word in edgewise. He turned the key, floored the pedal, and squealed out of the parking spot, moving once again away from the prison. For now.

He'd be back soon enough.

CHAPTER THREE

Ilse hurried up the stairs to the four-story Seattle field office. Her fingers tapped against her pocket where her phone sat—the same phone where she'd received the text message. Apparently, they'd been trying to reach her for a half-hour.

She winced. Dumb phones didn't allow her to put someone on hold. Work had tried to call, and she'd kept the line busy waiting for that stupid prison official.

The thought of Supervising Agent Rawley's look of disapproval hastened her steps up the stairs, leaving the metal detectors and security checkpoints behind.

A case. A new case; that's what the text had said.

She reached the top of the stairs and faced a room like any old office complex. Many cubicles, computers, gray foam dividers with black metal trim. Beyond the room and the clacking of keyboards or mutter of phone calls, Ilse spotted a lanky figure slinking through glass doors on the opposite side of the room.

She brightened. Agent Tom Sawyer had been called in as well.

She hastened around the edge of the room, feeling her anxiety rising. To keep it at bay, she muttered her memory trick, "Brown hair. Brown eyes. Forty-two. Thirty victims. Forty-six. November twenty-fourth." It didn't quite calm her, but it did help keep the unease in check.

As she drew nearer to the glass-walled office, she noted Sawyer facing Agent Rawley. The two men eyed each other like sniffing hounds, eyes alert and attentive for any threat. The men didn't much like each other, but they worked together well enough.

Rawley was the consummate professional, plus a bit of a health nut. Even now, he stood behind his standing desk, wearing his neat, perfectly maintained suit. His hair was combed, not a single strand out of place.

Sawyer, on the other hand, wore jeans, a flannel shirt, and a baseball cap.

Ilse brushed her hair past her ear and entered the office, the glass door swinging shut behind her without a sound.

"Glad you could make it," Rawley called over his desk, his piercing blue-gray eyes fixating on her.

Ilse winced, holding up an apologetic hand. Rawley turned to Sawyer. "You took your time getting here."

"Wasn't home," Sawyer said with a grunt.

Rawley hesitated. "Where were you?"

For anyone else this might have seemed like a prying question. But Ilse knew Sawyer like Rawley did. The man was married to his job. His last actual marriage was currently in the middle of a divorce-filing. For him to be out and about *doing* anything separate from work was cause for some concern.

Sawyer just shrugged. "Bird-watching."

"Oh," Rawley brightened. "I didn't know you were a birdwatcher. What's your favorite outlook? Have you seen the one at the arboretum?"

Sawyer scratched his chin, let out a weary sigh then said, "So... we have a case?"

Rawley straightened, clearing his throat and nodding. "Yes—yes of course." He reached out with a perfectly manicured, but unpainted hand, and flipped his computer screen on the standing desk. Two photos displayed on the screen.

"Two victims," Rawley said, "In the same area, found in two separate scrapyards."

"Scrapyards?" Sawyer said.

"Yes," Rawley replied. "And before you ask, no—someone wasn't trying to hide the bodies. That's why we're in—the bodies were meant to be found."

He clicked his mouse and the images changed to crime scene photos. Ilse winced, her fingers going suddenly still where they'd been tapping against her phone. Sawyer frowned, leaning in.

"Is that an old hydraulic press?" Sawyer asked, studying the first picture.

Rawley sniffed. "Possibly. That shape caught *under* it is our first victim."

Sawyer pointed at the screen. "Why are his hands over his head like that?"

"He was posed that way. The killer fancies himself a craftsman of sorts. Both victims were posed with wires and spikes."

Ilse regarded the second photo and felt her stomach sink. At first glance, the figure looked like he was driving a car, but on closer inspection she spotted the spike through the back of the headrest and the wire around the wrists, securing the hands to the steering wheel.

She looked away, feeling her stomach turn. Sawyer was far better at this part of the job. Ilse was still new to this sort of thing. She preferred dealing with survivors, not studying the pictures of victims. She let out a long breath and said, “Were they killed on site?”

Rawley began to answer, but Sawyer cut in. “No. Not enough blood,” he said. “They were killed elsewhere then posed there.”

Ilse wrinkled her nose. “Posed in junkyards? Why... not exactly the most foot traffic if you're trying to display something.”

“Might be the point,” Sawyer said with a grunt.

Rawley's eyes bounced between them both and he gave an approving nod, rotating his computer once more. “The first crime scene has been cleared. The body is gone from the second, but everything else has been left untouched. Thank you, agents.” He let out a faint sigh, and in a more personable tone, he said. “Places like this are often outside of town. They're poorly watched, and many don't have security systems...”

Tom nodded slowly.

Ilse finished the thought. “If our killer is exhibiting a pattern, he can strike as many times as he wants without getting caught.”

“That's where you come in,” Rawley said. “Besides, seeing as this one is in our backyard, I'm counting on you two. Seattle has a bit of a reputation where serial killers are concerned, doesn't it?” He glanced towards Sawyer, and said, without an ounce of emotion to his voice. “Might be a good idea for you to do well on this one, Tom.” He didn't blink, didn't emote. But there was clearly something in his eyes. A threat? Sawyer was known for being a bit of a hothead on the job. He'd even punched Rawley once before. Ilse felt a flicker of concern as she glanced between the two men.

“What do you mean?” Ilse asked, trying to keep her tone even. “Is—is something going on?”

Rawley glanced at her, shaking his head once. “I,” he said slowly, “am slated to move on from this branch. They're looking for a replacement, actually.”

“Oh... well, congrats,” Ilse said, still uneasy.

He smiled, nodding once. “I also am expected to give a report of current employees.”

Ilse's face fell. “Oh...”

Rawley looked Sawyer dead in the eyes. “Do your best on this one,

Tom. Your closure rate is what you've got going for you. I believe in you. Good day, agents."

Sawyer was already turning, hands jammed in his jeans pockets as he marched out the door. Ilse shot an uncomfortable look back at the computer screen, grateful the images were turned away now. This added pressure wasn't going to help her nerves. The idea of Sawyer being removed as her partner was absolutely unacceptable. She supposed Rawley was right. Tom's closure rate made up for some of his failings in playing nice with others.

She let out a faint sigh, then hastened after Sawyer.

CHAPTER FOUR

Ilse shot askance glances at her partner, trying to gauge his mood as the city passed by in a blur of gray and they hastened towards the second, and still maintained, crime scene. With Tom, it was always difficult to tell what he was thinking. His expression for hungry matched the same one for happy. And while she suspected he experienced a broad range of emotions, he had mastered the poker face.

She'd had clients like him in the past, but none were nearly as committed to keeping their feelings so bottled up.

Sawyer sat behind the wheel of the car, using one of his long legs to steer. “What?” he said.

“Huh?”

“What?” he asked, shooting her a glance. His stubborn, green gaze fixed on her then moved back to the road.

“Nothing.”

“You're watching me,” he said.

“I'm not.”

“You are,” he replied. “You were watching me back at Rawley's office, too.”

“I—umm. Did you hear what he said at the end there?”

“I heard.”

“You're not... concerned?”

“Nah. Rawley is always talking about promotion. Job review or not—same stuff for me.”

Ilse blinked. She wasn't sure she shared the sentiment. They needed to solve this case if only to make sure no more constants in her life shifted like tectonic plates.

“For real, though,” he said, glancing at her. “Why do you keep staring? Not just back at the office. I have a zit?”

“No.”

“So what is it?”

“Umm—I think I'm in love.”

Sawyer's expression cracked into a grin. He shook his head, his sandy-hair swishing. “Har har. I'm good, doc. Are you?”

Ilse determinedly looked in any direction except Sawyer's. “I'm fine... I got in touch with the warden at my father's prison.

"Oh? Good chat?"

"I've got the date of the parole. Next week."

"Mhmm. Good to hear..."

Ilse shot him a sidelong glance but quickly returned her eyes to the road. "So... How are things with you?"

Sawyer sighed, shaking his head. "Fine. Good. How much longer until we get there?" He glanced at the GPS and answered his own question as if trying to simply fill the space between them with sound. "Only a few minutes. Not bad."

"No... not bad," Ilse said slowly.

Sawyer was acting strange. He'd been acting strange back in Rawley's office. He'd been acting strange on their last case. And now here he was acting strange again. Sawyer wasn't the type to open up, and Ilse didn't want to pry, but she knew it had something to do with his sister.

Beyond that, it was nearly impossible to tell.

But birdwatching? Tom Sawyer? Fat chance. He'd rather watch paint dry.

Briefly, she wondered if she ought to pry a bit further, to see if there was any part of him that might want her help. He clearly suffered from trauma after the horrible events with his little sister. He'd never dealt with the emotional wounds and had only allowed them to fester.

Classic avoidance. Ilse was trained in dealing with that sort of thing, and most of all, seeing Tom hurt like this only made her own heart pang. Her old mentor Dr. Mitchell always knew what to say to get people to open up.

But with Sawyer, Ilse knew an indirect approach would just sound like manipulation to him. A direct approach would get shut down.

She sighed, glancing at the GPS herself now.

After the case...

After the case she'd confront him about his odd behavior. She'd straight-up ask him if he wanted help. It wouldn't have to be her—that might be awkward. She knew professionals though. Maybe even Dr. Mitchell.

But for now, the case had to come first.

Rawley's words from earlier came back to her and she shivered in her seat. Isolated junkyards, minimal security, as many locations as the killer's heart desired. And by the looks of things, he was only just getting started.

***

Ilse frowned at the scrapyard as they moved between walls of stacked cars and abandoned containers. The partitions of crushed automobiles seemed anything *but* sturdy. Her fingers brushed nervously at her hair, and she moved in Sawyer's shadow in the direction of the yellow caution tape ahead of them.

A couple of police were standing near a fluttering band of caution tape, not the usual crime scene stuff, but traffic tape. Ilse guessed a place like this might have it in supply.

Sawyer raised a hand, gravel crunching beneath his boots as he approached the cops. Ilse lingered back, allowing the recalcitrant agent to take the lead. Normally, Sawyer allowed her to do the talking. Now, though, he came to a halt by the fluttering caution tape.

“'hlo,” Sawyer grunted.

The cops glanced between the two of them. A suspicious, hesitant look. Ilse sighed, reaching for her identification. Sawyer's baseball cap, flannel, and jeans didn't exactly scream fed. Then again, her long-sleeved sweater and slacks weren't agency standard either.

“FBI,” Sawyer added as if it were a passing thought. He nodded towards Ilse's raised hand displaying her ID.

The cops relaxed.

“This the scene?” Sawyer asked, nodding past them.

The two officers stepped back, gesturing over the fluttering yellow tape. One of them, an older man with a bit of a paunch, massaged his chin. He smelled like caffeine, though he'd managed to squirrel away any Styrofoam evidence before the feds had arrived.

“That car,” he said. “The one facing the wrong direction.”

“Buick?” Sawyer asked.

“Yup.”

The two men seemed to be on the same wavelength, communicating telepathically, using as few sentences as possible. Sawyer nodded in gratitude, and the older cop raised the tape, allowing the agents to duck underneath.

Ilse cautiously approached behind Sawyer. “No overgrowth,” she murmured, pointing.

Sawyer nodded. “Yeah. Saw that too. Car was moved here. Plates?”

“No plates,” Ilse said as she stepped to the side to check.

Sawyer nodded. “Serial is probably removed too. Worth checking.”

He approached the door, peering through a shattered window. He tentatively extended his hand towards the handle of the car, but then pulled up, frowning.

"What is that?" Ilse asked, studying the seam between the car door and the frame.

"Welding. Someone welded the door shut."

Ilse wrinkled her nose, staring at the melted, then cooled metal. Why go to so much work? Welding the door? She glanced at the others. The rest weren't melted. She glanced back at the front door, the shattered glass, her eyes flitting towards the blood stains on the headrest and steering wheel. A couple of wires, snipped now, still dangled where they had once secured the now absent body to the wheel.

Sawyer called over his shoulder. "Any prints? DNA?"

"None!" the old cop called back. He was sipping from a coffee thermos that had appeared as if from nowhere.

"Forensics been through?"

"Yup. Nothing found."

Sawyer scratched beneath his chin, glancing back at the car. "Well shit," he muttered. "Any thoughts, doc?"

Ilse studied the car a moment longer, then murmured. "He gets off on the fear. The posing, welding the door. It's like a screenwriter, holding anticipation until the final moment. He wanted someone to *see* the body, but not be able to do anything about it."

"So a sadist?"

"Probably."

"Great," Sawyer grunted. "It's always gotta be a sadist."

He did another lap of the car, while Ilse remained, frowning. The car was facing the wrong direction. An oversight by the killer? Intentional to draw the eye?

She looked away now, across the great expanse of the scrapyard. Rows of soon-to-be repurposed scraps and metal angled in alleys throughout the dusty space.

Rawley's words came back, along with shivers.

The killer had as many junkyards as he wanted to choose from. All generally remote, with few eyewitnesses. Plus, the welding, the metal spike, the soldered door—in a place like a scrapyard, he'd have all the toys to work with that his heart desired.

This guy was only just getting started.

Sawyer raised a hand, waving towards the cops again. "We got the witness who found the body?"

"Yup—he's in the office. Tough old guy. Wants to go home."

"Let's speak to him so he can," Ilse interjected, nodding. Crime scenes were Sawyer's realm of expertise. But people? That's where Ilse's experience came into play.

She ducked back under the caution tape, taking the lead this time as she hastened towards the indicated office building.

CHAPTER FIVE

The office building centered the junkyard, little more than a garage with windows and a wooden door that didn't quite fit its frame. Two of the windows had compliance letters, warnings, advertisements—and everything in between—plastered all over the glass.

The door creaked as Ilse tapped tentatively against the frame. "Hello?" she called. "FBI..."

"Come in!" A voice called to her. A gruff, rasping voice. A voice accustomed to cigarettes and shouting at trespassers.

As she pushed into the small space, she spotted the man who belonged to the voice. He matched perfectly.

The old scrapyard employee was still wearing his blue jumpsuit with a nametag on front that read "Samuel." His eyes were puffy, but it didn't look as if he'd been crying, more like his skin was loose from old age and lack of sleep.

Even as she entered the moldered office space, the man held a hand to his lips, yawning. The same hand then migrated to his short-cut, prickling pale hair which he stroked back.

Ilse heard the sound of boots against dust and gravel behind her, suggesting Sawyer was slowly making his way towards the office as well.

"Hello, Mr. Samuel," Ilse said nodding quickly. Rapport was often best established, in her experience, one on one. With Sawyer still behind her, introductions prompted an initial connection that might yield results in later lines of questioning. "My name is Dr. Beck," she said simply.

"Pleased to meet you, lady. You can call me Samuel. No mister."

"Alright, Samuel—I don't want to take up any more of your time."

His greasy, blue jumpsuit seemed perfectly at home in the dingy, moldered office-space. The floors alone were covered in dust and rust and mildew. The walls were soiled and the wallpaper curled from wet spots. Some of the water damage had been covered with posters and pictures of scantily clad women and monster trucks.

Samuel was standing by the chair near a desk. Still standing. Ilse admired that. He was a tough old cookie.

"You sure you're a cop?" he said, scratching at his elbow.

"I—pardon?"

"Kinda pretty to be a cop. No makeup, neither." He pointed at her face. "Office-types all wear makeup."

"I—I just don't..." Ilse blinked, taken aback. Her training kicked in, though. Impudent questions were often meant to rattle. Sometimes used as a way of testing mettle. So instead of reacting, she just nodded, smiling, then volleyed back one of her own. "You found the body?"

He winced but nodded. "Eight hours ago. My shift was up at five."

"Like I said, very sorry to keep you here. Did anything stand out about the body when you found it?"

"It was dead."

Sawyer, who'd joined them now, standing in the doorway, hid an amused chuckle.

Ilse continued. "I suppose that *would* stand out. Did you know the victim?"

"Nope," he said, seemingly having attended the same school of communication skills as Sawyer and the old cop.

For someone whose career dealt in words, Ilse was practically starving. She tried again. "Any ideas how he got in?"

The man shrugged. "Not much security here. Few old locks on a fence. Some barbed wire. Most the wire though has been stolen anyway." He snorted, his eyes twinkling. "Kinda funny. Put up wire to stop people stealing metal. Then the metal thieves just take the wire. Ha."

Sawyer hid another chuckle.

Ilse resisted the urge to roll her eyes. "So this place has poor security? Any cameras?"

He snorted. "Hell no. They'd just take the cameras."

"Do people often steal from scrapyards?"

"Sort of like a rite of passage for some kids. But also old, broken things—people don't see them the same way. Don't think of it as stealing."

"Wouldn't cameras prevent that?"

"Nah. Not worth it. The things *really* worth taking are too heavy for them to cart out anyhow. Besides, that's why Ben hires me. I keep an eye on the place at night."

Ilse could feel her frustration mounting. "Is there anything you think could be helpful?" She waited, wincing half in anticipation.

But perhaps predictably, the old junkyard employee simply grunted,

"Nope."

Sawyer tapped Ilse on the shoulder. "Coroner's office is ready," he muttered. "Nothing else to see here."

She sighed but nodded. "Thank you Mr—er, Samuel. I appreciate your time."

"Can I go sleep now?"

"At your convenience."

Ilse allowed Sawyer to lead her from the old, rotten office space. She was grateful for the fresh morning air, beneath the sunlight as they moved away from the space, back up the old road towards where they'd parked outside the metal gates.

"Nothing," Ilse murmured as they moved. "No prints. No DNA. No witness. Samuel didn't see anything."

"You think he had something to do with it?"

"I—I was wondering, but no. Why report his own crime? Why do it at his own workplace? Besides, no reason to think he did. Old guy like that? The murder stage took some doing."

Sawyer nodded, tipping his cap. "Thought so, too. Coroner might have something."

Ilse nodded, rubbing at her arms in a nervous, fidgeting gesture. "Let's hope so. Because right now, we've got absolutely nothing."

***

Ilse missed the warmth of the sunshine as she stepped into the cold coroner's office that shared the basement of a day-clinic. An older woman, with beautiful, curling hair sat on a tall, three-legged stool, a clipboard in one hand, the eraser on a pencil chewed between her teeth.

She glanced at the agents as they drew near. "Tom Sawyer? Ilse Beck?" she said as if reading a roster.

"That's us," Sawyer said. "What you got? Also, where's your boss?"

"Vacation. I'm authorized to offer input, though, on behalf of the office."

Sawyer shrugged. "Shoot. What input you got?"

The coroner gestured with the chewed end of her pencil towards a gurney with a white blanket. And then gestured towards the large, refrigerator compartments behind the gurney. "Your two victims were killed by blunt-force trauma."

"Head wounds?"

"Relatively painless. Which, I guess might be a relief given the condition their bodies were in."

Ilse felt her stomach churn. This was the one of her least favorite parts of the job. She gritted her teeth, forcing herself to listen, like someone just waiting for a roller coaster ride to stop.

"So most the wounds were made afterwards?" Sawyer asked.

"It seems so. But there wasn't enough blood at the crime scene."

"Yeah," Sawyer replied. "Killed elsewhere, right?"

"It looks that way." The woman's curls bounced as she nodded her head and tapped her pencil against the wooden edge of her clipboard. "They were bludgeoned, transported, then their bodies... well, you've seen the photos. I can show you again if you'd like."

Ilse looked away, thinking she might be sick.

Sawyer said. "Piercings in the wrists. Head. Parts of the abdomen."

She nodded. "That's right. Also, most of the injuries were done with a bias towards the right side of the victims' bodies."

Sawyer frowned. "What does that mean?"

Ilse murmured, "He's left-handed."

The coroner tapped her nose and pointed towards Ilse. "I can't be certain, but it's definitely possible our killer prefers his left. Or maybe he just wants us to think that."

"Biased towards the right," Sawyer said with a puff of air. "A left-handed sadist. I mean... might help narrow things a bit." The coroner beamed, nodding quickly. Ilse detected the note of sarcasm but didn't comment. "Anything else? DNA? Semen? Blood?"

"Nothing from the killer, I'm afraid," the coroner said. "He was careful. Plus, the fact that the body was moved from another scene contaminated most potential physical evidence."

Sawyer turned away now, studying Ilse. "Got any thoughts about this left-handed sadist of ours?"

"We don't know he's left-handed," Ilse corrected. "Maybe he's just throwing us off. He did move the bodies."

"Maybe. I mean... guess we can talk with the victim's dad. Rawley said they were coming down to the office to meet up. Give a statement."

Ilse winced. Grief, though, didn't bother her nearly so much as blood. She'd experienced enough of it in her own life. Part of her felt equipped to help those struggling with sorrow.

"Alright, let's talk to the family," she said.

CHAPTER SIX

Tom leaned in the doorway of the interrogation room, his shoulder not quite allowing the large, steel frame to close. He didn't want Mr. Wagonmaker to feel trapped. The man wasn't a suspect.

Tom's motive was partly altruistic. But also, a door open at his back gave him an escape route.

In situations like these, dealing with grieving parents, Sawyer preferred to let Ilse take the lead. He'd been told in the past that his bedside manner was somewhat lacking. Not that he minded. Ilse had been trained in this sort of thing.

Sawyer leaned in the doorframe of the interrogation room, watching as Ilse worked her magic. Dr. Beck's hand reached across the table in a comforting gesture, her fingers not quite actually touching Mr. Wagonmaker. Ilse had even thought to bring tissues, which she'd snatched from the night-sergeant's desk. These she extended to the tearful father of the latest victim.

In a way, it was like watching a ju-jitsu practitioner go through their motions. Ilse knew what to say, how to respond, how to comfort in most situations. Even now, watching, he noted the way she mirrored Mr. Wagonmaker's posture. Slumped shoulders, weary sighs, somber tone.

Ilse genuinely cared about these people. It's what made her so good at this part of the job. Sawyer, on the other hand, tried his best to care.

But his motivation had always been the same: find the bad guy and lock him up.

He felt his lips twitch, threatening to turn into a sneer. He caught the gesture, keeping his face impassive. Lock *most* of them up. The monster behind *those* particular gray walls didn't deserve a jail cell—he deserved a coffin.

"I'm very sorry sir," Ilse was busy saying, her voice laden with compassion. "I didn't realize he was only nineteen."

Mr. Wagnomaker sniffed, gratefully accepting one of the tissues Ilse had provided. He dabbed at his eyes but nodded. "Was going off to college this fall," he said. "I—I can't even imagine how scared he must have been."

The second victim's father was short but athletically built. His jaw was chiseled, due, most likely, to an impressively disciplined diet and workout regime. He wore glasses, but these were now resting on the table as he dabbed at his eyes.

"Did your son know anyone by the name of Janet Lee?"

He looked up, sniffing. "Who?"

Ilse slid a picture across the desk of the first victim. The one who'd been trapped beneath the hydraulic press. The picture she showed, of course, was only from a driver's license.

Mr. Wagonmaker stared at the image, his brow furrowing. "I—I who is this?"

"You don't recognize her?"

"No—no did she have something to do with—"

"No sir," Ilse said quickly. "She was another victim."

This comment elicited another huff of air as the trim man tried to control his emotions. "I don't know her," he said at last. "Never seen her in my life."

Ilse leaned back, folding her hands over each other. "And Matthew's mother..." she let the unspoken question linger.

"Not in the picture. Hasn't been for more than a decade. I raised Matty myself."

Tom's stomach twisted at this comment. He thought of his own father, thought of his sister... The pain that killers caused could never be undone. Ilse seemed to think she could talk people into some version of health. Some way to heal their emotions, their hurting. But watching Mr. Wagonmaker, Agent Sawyer didn't believe it.

"Did anyone have a grudge against Matty?" Ilse said, using the pet name the father had. "I know it's tough to think about, but anything you can remember will help."

The victim's father hiccupped but shook his head. "Nothing like that. Everyone liked Matty."

"What type of car did he drive?" Sawyer chimed in from the doorway.

Both Ilse and the father looked towards him blinking in surprise as if they'd forgotten he was even there.

"I—car?" Mr. Wagonmaker said.

Tom nodded. "Not a Buick, was it?" he thought back to the totaled junkyard vehicle where the body had been posed. They'd been careful about not filling the father in on *too* many of the details. Just enough to help the case, but not so much to give him nightmares for the rest of his life.

"No—no Matty didn't drive," Mr. Wagonmaker said, shaking his head.

Sawyer and Ilse both zeroed in on this comment, their heads swiveling at the same time. "Why not?" they both said simultaneously.

The father looked somewhat taken aback by the force of the query. He cleared his throat, hesitantly.

"What I mean to say," Ilse amended quickly, in a gentler tone, "is it's somewhat unusual for a nineteen-year-old boy to *not* drive. Did he have his license?"

"Yes, yes. He had that, but Matty was in a terrible accident a couple of years ago. When he first started driving. It—it was somewhat Matt's fault, but no one was too hurt in the accident."

Sawyer focused on the man now, eyes narrowed. "What type of accident?"

"Umm. Vehicle?"

Ilse said, "I think we're more wondering the degree of damage to the cars."

"Oh. Mattie's car was totaled. He was devastated. I'd given it to him as a gift on his sixteenth birthday..." Mr. Wagonmaker trailed off again and ducked his head at the recollection, reaching for the tissue box once more.

"You're sure no one was hurt in the wreck?" Sawyer asked.

Ilse shot him a disapproving glance, gesturing towards the tissues. Sawyer shrugged and sighed. He turned, slipping into the hall and allowing the door to shut behind him. He'd heard enough. Besides, it was starting to get late—all the red tape had sapped half their day.

None of this could be a coincidence. The kid who'd been killed had also been in an automobile accident only a couple years prior, and then they found him in a junkyard in a totaled car?

It meant something.

They just had to figure out what.

CHAPTER SEVEN

He thought of himself as a survivor. And this place, this *home* he had made for himself, was testament to things that survived.

The floor creaked beneath him as he moved across the old, worn floorboards. Part of his home had once been an outhouse. Another part a repurposed shed. And now, it was his estate.

In one corner of the room was a coffee maker that had been discarded. It worked perfectly fine. They simply hadn't understood the wiring.

In another part of his small space, there was a workbench. Half the bench had been made from discarded lumber. But a little bit of time, and elbow grease, and he'd resurrected this as well.

An ornate chandelier, with a few of the dangling, glass baubles missing, illuminated his place. This also had been found discarded. Refuse redeemed.

He smiled, moving across the room towards the front door. He pushed it open, listening to the satisfying groan of the hinges. The sound of metal. He didn't grease the door. Didn't see the point.

Why hide what metal was?

He stood in his doorway, peering out across the abandoned junkyard. Other scavengers had been through, taking what they had wanted. He had to chase off more than one with a rusted bat.

But for the most part, this place was left without visitors. A hazard sign on the gates saw to that. A few years ago, it had been intended for demolition, for the remaining scraps to be carted off to other junkyards. But litigation had caused that plan to delay.

When they wanted to, government officials knew how to conjure as much red tape as they wanted.

As he pushed open the door and checked the position of the sun in the sky, he murmured to himself, "Two hours. Not longer. Yeah, yeah I definitely think so." He tilted his head, wrinkling his nose as if listening to a question. Then he shook his head. "Why would I do that? Whatever."

He chuckled at a joke, smirking. He tried to close the door, slowly, but the wind caught it. He tried to catch it with his other hand.

No. That would never have been possible.

Pain shot up his right side. He winced, gritting his teeth and pressing his forehead against the rough wood of the door.

He was a survivor. The pain was his friend. It made him stronger; wasn't that what the good book said? The Almighty disciplined those he loved. The survivor had endured more than his share of discipline.

Others thought they were like him. But time quickly showed otherwise. That girl, who'd survived that work accident four years ago, she hadn't made it this time. And what about that teenage boy? The one who had walked away from an accident that would've killed most. He'd been unscathed.

Now, though, he wasn't walking around, bragging about it. He wasn't walking at all.

No, there was only one survivor. The machines saw to it.

He glanced shiftily about his room, eyes on the coffee maker. He left it unplugged. This machine was particularly harmless.

But his own experience, his own accident, not so long ago, proved what he knew intuitively. *Everything* could be dangerous.

"How often do we take it for granted, hmm?" He sighed, shaking his head and answering his own question. "Too damn often," he whispered. "These things won't solve our problems. They never have!"

He stared suddenly towards the picture of the man above his sink. The sink was made from an old pipe cut lengthwise with a hole in the center. The picture, though, was kept pristine. No splatter marks, no water damage. The picture was all he had left...

Other pictures, of the same image, sat in a stack on his bookshelf. He'd made the shelf, too.

He didn't keep the pictures out of love, nor to commemorate. No... The picture was of the man he hated most in the world. The one that got away...

The one that quite *literally* got away. Had escaped. Before the survivor could do anything. Before the survivor could make him pay for all this damn pain.

He snarled, reaching out and ripping the picture from the wall. He placed it beneath his sink, turning the water on, and watching the liquid pound that stupid face. A work photo from the website. A photo before the bastard had gone and gotten himself killed, before the survivor could take sweet revenge.

Now all he had was pixels and paper.

Once the picture had soaked through, he ripped it to shreds, tossing it in the trash.

Then, deftly, he moved over to the bookshelf, reached up and grabbed another picture. Identical to the last one. With a sigh, he walked over to the sink again. And once more, he stuck this new image in its proper place.

He glared at the figure. He had printed thousands of these things. And now he was running low. He'd have to go back for a new batch.

"You're lucky I never got my hands on you," the killer whispered, staring at the photo over the sink. But even as he said these words, he felt a surge of fury. "Not that I ever could have, now could I? Thanks to you. I hope you rot in hell."

He turned away, feeling a spike of anger, of rage. Sometimes he burned the photos. Other times he drowned them. Once, he'd used battery acid. It didn't completely reduce the urge.

But it helped.

All he had was the pictures... and the others. He'd taken a big step in going after bleeders. But someone had to pay.

He'd survived. Others didn't. Besides, he already knew who he was going to visit next.

He smiled to himself, holding a quiet conference in his mind. He nodded, and muttered, "Couple more hours. Maybe a bit more. Yeah, that sounds about right."

He winced as another jolt of pain went down his right side. He tested his right arm with his left hand, letting out a hiss of pain.

Sometimes, the pain became almost unbearable. Sometimes, the only way he could release it was to inflict it on others.

And the episodes were getting longer. The pain worse. He couldn't wait much longer.

He already had his next target chosen.

CHAPTER EIGHT

"I don't like being back here while it's getting late," Ilse grumbled, frowning through the window as they maneuvered back into the parking lot outside Ben Connolly's scrapyard.

"You have a better idea?" Tom asked.

Ilse sighed and shook her head. She reclined in the car seat, staring towards the towers of crushed automobiles, metal containers, scraps, and old appliances. She paid particular attention to the rusted, metal gate as they passed through.

Sawyer came to a complete halt just inside, pulling off to the edge of the road. He parked, pushed open the door, one lanky leg jutting out into the dirt. He looked back at her. "This is the same shift when Matthew was discovered. These guys were all here when the car was pulled into the lot and the body was posed."

Ilse shivered, shaking her head. "I still can't believe none of them saw anything."

Sawyer nodded. "It *is* hard to believe."

Ilse glanced down at her phone, alerted by a faint vibration.

Sawyer quirked an eyebrow. "Social call?"

Ilse studied the text. It simply read, *Nothing today. Sorry.*

Ilse sighed, shaking her head. "No, my neighbor. I asked them to check my mail for me while I was gone."

Sawyer still remained half inside the car. "Your neighbor? Who is he?"

Ilse shot Tom a look. "*She*," Ilse said "is keeping an eye out for postcards."

"Ah, right. Gotcha. No new cards?"

Ilse had vaguely told Tom about thc postcards. He didn't know the extent. If anything, he sounded more relieved to find out her neighbor was a woman than that there had been no more postcards. As for Ilse, she wasn't as relieved. Without a new postcard, she didn't have any more clues. As Sawyer slipped out of the car, into the junkyard, he raised his hand to greet a man in a blue jumpsuit heading their way.

The jumpsuit reminded her of her father's own ensemble back in the prison when she'd visited him. She still needed to book a ticket. Part of her wanted to rehearse what she was going to say. No number of entreaties or begging would suffice to keep that man behind bars. She watched through the glass, as Sawyer approached the night shift junkyard employee.

She closed her phone, jamming it into her pocket. "Focus," she muttered to herself.

There would be time for postcards and parents on parole later. Now they had a case to solve.

She pushed out of the car, hurrying up towards Sawyer where she caught words from the employee. "Don't know nothing about that," the man was saying, shaking his head. He had an average sized body, but a very wide face. It almost looked as if any extra calories went directly to his jowls. His double chin wagged as he said, insistently, "None of us saw nothing."

"You were here last night?" Sawyer replied.

The junkyard employee shrugged. "Yes. Did our job. I left."

"How many of you are there on shift right now?"

The man shrugged, pulling out a greasy rag from his pocket and dabbing at sweat drops on his forehead. "Well, let's see. There's me." He nodded, as if confirming he was present. "There's Samuel. He stays later. And there's the boss."

Ilse frowned. "Just the three of you?"

The man glanced back at her. He rubbed with the same sweaty and greasy cloth at the back of his neck. "Not many people come through this late at night. Fact, you two are the first in the last hour."

Ilse glanced back towards the rusted gate. There were holes in the fence everywhere. Barbed wire on top of a few of the posts was absent from many others. Further along, near a junk pile, it looked like part of the metal mesh was missing completely.

She looked back at the employee. "You didn't see anything at all last night? *Nothing*?"

He shifted uncomfortably, glancing over his shoulder towards the office, then back again. "Nothing. Nothing at all. Very sad what happened to that boy. But no one here had anything to do with it."

Ilse jammed her hands in her pockets. "So you say..." She frowned, marching past Sawyer, and moving towards the office once again.

She knew she hadn't liked that office. One could tell a lot about someone by how they kept their private space. The junkyard workers didn't spend as much time in the office as their boss. Ben, if she remembered last night's exchange with Samuel.

But Ben Connolly didn't run a tight ship. His junkyard was run like junk. In a way it was almost fitting. But in another way, it allowed Ilse a glimpse into the mind of someone who didn't take the job very seriously. Perhaps someone who resented the job, maybe even society?

"He's not there," a voice called out.

She paused, glancing back. "Who's not where?"

The employee waved a hand towards the office. "The boss. He's not in there."

Ilse shot a look at Sawyer, and he cleared his throat. "What makes you think we were going to speak with the boss?"

The employee just shrugged. "Only two other people here. You already spoke with Samuel yesterday. I ain't dumb."

Ilse shrugged. Sawyer nodded. The man made a point.

Sawyer said, "I thought your boss was going to be here. We requested that everyone who worked the same shift last night be present."

The man with the thick neck shook his head. "I don't know what happened. He called in. Said he couldn't make it."

Ilse frowned now. "Why?"

"Don't know. He's the boss. If he doesn't want to come in, he doesn't have to."

Ilse pointed over her shoulder towards the office. "When we asked you about anything you wanted to share, you glanced back that way. Why?"

The man stuttered. "Is there a crime against looking?"

"No. Except up until that point you were focused on me. And then on Tom. It was only when we asked you something you didn't want to answer that you looked away. And your eyes went in that direction. You tried to pretend like you were staring at those cars. But your subconscious first directed you towards your boss's office. Why?"

The man just looked stunned. He gaped at her. Sawyer grunted, "She does that sometimes. Might as well tell the truth."

The man wiped at his face again, then said, "Really, it's nothing."

"What's nothing?"

"Just, the boss came in late yesterday too. He comes in at all hours. Like I said, he owns the place. Has keys for everything. Access everywhere."

Ilse crossed her arms. "So two days he's been weird with the schedule?"

"I'm saying he wasn't here. He couldn't dump a body if he *wasn't* here." The man nodded adamantly as if this proved it.

Ilse frowned. "Any guesses why he might not be here?"

"I don't want to guess."

Sawyer said, "Try. Or maybe you can come with us down to the station and try there."

The man's hands jutted up, as greasy as his handkerchief. "Hang on. No need to take me anywhere. I've got to watch the kids tonight."

Sawyer just nodded at him, with an encouraging little flick of his fingers.

"Fine. Fine. A guess? My guess is he's taking care of his sister. She's needed some help since, well, all that horrible business about a year ago."

Again, in perfect synchronization, Ilse and Tom both said, "What happened a year ago?"

His eyes darted between the two of them, like pale orbs beneath the night. "Nothing much. Nothing he did. A horrible accident. His niece, in a car crash. Sometimes his sister just needs help. It's been tough for her." He muttered beneath his breath, shaking his head. "I really shouldn't be talking about this. Doesn't feel right."

Ilse and Tom, though, were both shooting each other knowing looks.

"A car crash," Tom said, quietly. "Interesting."

Ilse said, "You don't happen to have an address for this boss of yours, do you?"

"His address or his sister's?"

Ilse considered it, then said, "*His*."

"It's on the Rolodex in the office. But I really don't think you should be—"

Ilse was already moving up the dusty road towards the office. Tom followed quickly after her.

CHAPTER NINE

Ilse and Sawyer drove beneath a busted streetlight, both of them quiet, both of them fixated on the small house at the end of the block.

The junkyard owner didn't live in a particularly nice part of town. Already, Ilse had heard two gunshots.

She shivered, murmuring her memory trick beneath her breath as they moved slowly down the street, trying not to attract attention. A couple of pedestrians eyed them suspiciously.

"Shouldn't have driven such a new car," Sawyer muttered.

"Yeah? That scrapyard employee didn't seem in the lending mood," she replied. "Look, the garage is opening."

Ilse's eyes darted to the GPS, then towards the garage next to the tiny, single-story house. Indeed, Connolly's car was pulling out of the driveway. Ilse read the license plate, and said, "That's his. He's home."

"Taking care of his sister my ass," Tom muttered.

The two of them lingered back, allowing the rusted, junker of a car, put together from various pieces judging by the paint job, pull onto the road ahead of them and begin to move through the dingy part of town.

"Pull him over or follow?" Sawyer muttered.

Ilse hesitated, then said, "Follow, I think. Maybe he's going out for another victim."

The two of them went quiet again, trundling slowly through the streets. As they tailed at a distance, over rough roads, beneath streetlights which were mostly flickering or broken completely, the buildings only grew more worn down. Some of them now had boards instead of windows. Everything had graffiti. There was more movement of pedestrians on street corners. Ilse glimpsed as money exchanged hands through a vehicle window near an alley, and a small black box was traded for the cash.

"I think that's a drug deal," Ilse muttered.

Sawyer said, "Probably a weapon. The box was too big. Money too much."

Ilse winced.

They trundled past the street corner, and Ilse didn't allow herself to stare.

They weren't here for arms dealing or drugs. They were here to catch a killer. "Where's he going?" she murmured.

The old, multicolored car ahead of them turned down a smaller street.

Tom hesitated, fingers tensed. “If we follow,” the sandy-haired agent murmured, “he might make us.”

Ilse bit her lip, considering their options. Suddenly, the lights from the car dimmed. The alley fell in darkness once again.

“Pull over,” Ilse said urgently. “We can follow on foot!”

Sawyer nodded, guiding their sedan to the side of the road, parking next in front of a boarded-up bar. He shut the vehicle off, making sure they were out of sight from the alley. He then slipped out of the car, waited for Ilse, and both shut their doors quietly.

Tom locked the doors and then took the lead with that lanky gait of his, unbuttoning his holster. Ilse, who never liked carrying her weapon, untucked her sweater, giving her access. As she followed after the baseball-cap wearing agent into the alley, she muttered her memory trick beneath her breath. They stepped beneath a fire-escape, the scent of refuse lingering on the air. Under the evening sky, the shadows from the flanking buildings practically swallowed the alley.

Ilse's gaze skipped across an abandoned couch, towards the far side of the space. The junkyard boss's dilapidated car was parked, wedged in the dark. But he was moving ahead of the vehicle towards where a metal door was open in the back of a greasy, worn-down building.

Sawyer slipped alongside the parked car, still moving quietly, hunched as he went. Ilse followed, wrinkling her nose as her back slid along the grimy wall.

“You got it?” a voice muttered from further ahead.

A new figure entered the alley, stepping onto a concrete slab stoop, through the open metal door. The figure wore a dark hood low over their face. The orange, glowing end of a cigarette temporarily illuminated a haggard visage, but then a puff of smoke clouded the man's eyes. “I got it,” the figure said, their voice slurred around their smoke.

Ilse and Tom had gone still, frozen by the car, pressed against the wall, hidden by shadow and cloud.

Ilse watched, her breathing regulated, as an envelope appeared in the hand of the man in the hooded sweater. He extended it towards the scrapyard boss. Mr. Connolly accepted the envelope, but immediately opened it. There was the sound of shuffling paper.

"It's all there," the hooded figure snapped.

"Trust but verify," Connolly replied.

An uneasy, tentative silence lingered. Then, the scrapyard boss snorted, raising the envelope. "What's this?" he demanded. "You're a stack short!"

"What? Nah—nah man. All there!"

"You trying to cheat me, you little runt! We had a deal!"

Sawyer hissed, "Time to go." He pulled his weapon and broke into a jog. "Stop there!" Sawyer called, his voice booming. "FBI!"

"Shit!" cursed the man in the door, he spun on his heel and disappeared back inside. He yanked the door shut behind him. The metal lock clicked. Ilse winced, briefly glancing towards the door, but they were here to catch the killer. Nothing else. She returned her attention to their suspect.

Mr. Connolly was cursing, his fingers scrambling at the door. He dropped his envelope and a stack of bills fluttered to the ground.

He doubled over, scrambling to pick them up, then turned on his heel and bolted, throwing himself at a fire escape, trying to pull himself up.

He slipped once, twice, but then managed to grip the lowest rung of a ladder.

"Hey! Stop it!" Sawyer shouted.

Ilse and Tom hastened forward, weapons drawn, footsteps tapping rapidly up the concrete floor.

The junkyard owner tried to yank himself up the fire escape with a grunt, but Sawyer lunged, snaring his foot and pulling hard.

The two men collapsed in a tangle. It took a second, but Sawyer managed to get on top. "Stop it!" Sawyer snapped. "Stop kicking! Hands where I can see them—hands!"

Ilse kept her distance, her weapon angled off. She pulled her cuffs from her pocket as she stepped over a pile of hundred-dollar-bills. She handed the cuffs to Sawyer who hastily subdued their suspect and dragged him to his feet.

"It wasn't anything!" Connolly shouted. "Was paying for cello lessons!"

"Tell me downtown," Sawyer muttered, shoving the man towards their waiting car.

CHAPTER TEN

Under good lightning, Mr. Connolly looked far less like a threatening thug and far more like a nervous substitute teacher with a yellowish combover. His hands twisted nervously at each other, rattling the cuffs. He seemed to forget his range of motion was restricted and kept trying to reach up to brush his hair out of his eyes, but inevitably just jerked his other hand thanks to the chain.

This process repeated a few times while Ilse watched him curiously.

Sawyer, as he often did, was standing in the interrogation room, pacing behind the chair of Mr. Connolly.

Ilse sat upright across the table from their suspect. She glanced down at the printed information in front of her, cleared her throat, then said, "It doesn't look good for you, Ben. Do you mind if I call you Ben?"

"Sure—sure whatever. I swear that money was for cello lessons. It wasn't what it looked like."

"Sure," Ilse replied in the same intonation he'd used. "Cello lessons. That's why you met someone in a dark alley and why you tried to run when we shouted FBI."

"I—it was a mistake."

Sawyer grunted. "Just like the mistake you made back at your junkyard? How about the mistake you made with that hydraulic press?"

As Sawyer said it, Ilse studied Mr. Connolly. His brow furrowed in confusion. He shot a look over his shoulder but couldn't turn completely. He reached up to comb his hair but only ended up jerking his wrists again. "Shit," he muttered. "Christ—what? What hydraulic... At my yard? What about my yard?"

"You were missing yesterday," Tom said, circling the table.

"I—no, that's not right. I was there. Early on." The man tried to touch his face again, and again winced as the cuffs went taut.

"We have a reliable source that says you didn't show up later on—around the time the body was found."

"Shit—what? Jerome's spreading lies, isn't he? That no good piece of—"

"I'd worry more about how it looks for you than your employee."

Mr. Connolly shifted uncomfortably, shaking his head in frustration. “Man, I don't know what you're talking about. I didn't—I had some business to take care of!”

“More cello lessons?” Ilse said in a would-be innocent voice.

The scrapyard owner faded off into dark muttering, shaking his head and looking off to the side now. At last, he looked up. “I'm no killer,” he said.

“Sure,” Tom replied. He didn't sound sure at all.

“I'm not! I swear it.”

“I'm convinced,” Tom said.

“Damn it, man, look. Okay. The money was for some favors. Letting some... you know, *organized* types move some of their stuff... You know?”

“You keep saying that,” Tom replied, still pacing. “But no, I don't know. How about you spit it out before I arrest you for double homicide.”

Connolly's face went as white as a sheet. “D-double... Shit man, no! There ain't no double... What? No—no. Look, I just let them park some cars. Move some merchandise.”

Ilse leaned in. “Organized, you said... Like the mob?”

He shot her a shifty-eyed glance and even lowered his voice, hissing a whisper. “Careful how loud you say that,” he muttered. “It wasn't anything. I just left some chains off gates. Let them enter late at night. You know—a pretty sweet deal. And no one got hurt!”

“No one got hurt,” Sawyer said. “So you're telling us that you worked out a deal with the mob to help them move stolen cars and goods at your scrapyard?”

“I—well...” He sighed. “I wouldn't say I knew exactly *what* they were moving.”

“What were the terms of this deal?” Sawyer demanded.

“Man—no questions asked. You can't ask questions of guys like that. They just wanted, you know, a little space. And they helped me keep the lights on.”

Ilse said, “I spotted quite a few hundred-dollar notes than needed for an electrical bill.”

Tom snorted, running a hand through his hair. “So you're saying you intentionally leave your gates unlocked... Shit,” he muttered, turning away in disgust.

Ilse winced. “You think the mob is behind those bodies?” she asked.

Sawyer looked at her. “Dunno. Could be. Sending a message?”

Ilse hesitated, considering it. “M-maybe... just, while it's possible, I guess a local crime ring wouldn't want to show off their murders. They'd want to hide them and let other criminals know—as a warning, but not cops. We found those bodies quick.”

“Man, man, man,” Mr. Connolly was saying, having finally learned how to coordinate his wrists to hold his head in his hands. “Shit... Shit. Shit. Those guys must've done this! Yeah—easily could've been them...”

Sawyer and Ilse shared a look, then returned their attention to the scrapyard owner. “How about you make an introduction,” Sawyer said. “Might help clear your own name.”

“An—a what?”

“You heard me.”

“I—I can't, man. You know what they'll do if a couple of feds show up, sniffing around?”

“Huh, well, probably not worse than two life sentences. Wachoo think?”

Ilse winced sympathetically, weathering the storm of more stuttering. At last, Mr. Connolly slammed his hands against the table. “I, I can arrange a meeting with my contact from the organization tomorrow morning. Bright in the morning. In a very public place. Just—you know, go light... Don't arrest nobody.”

“No promises,” Sawyer said. “Besides, you can cool your heels here tonight. Just so we can keep an eye on you.”

“Man—you believe me, don't you? I didn't kill no one!”

Sawyer didn't reply, already moving towards the door. Ilse pushed to her feet, shot a final look towards their suspect, sighed, and followed after the green-eyed agent.

The two of them reconvened in the hall as the interrogation room door shut behind them with a soft, ominous *click.*

Sawyer looked at Ilse in the dark hall. “Thoughts?”

She shook her head. “I'm not sure. He doesn't seem like a sadist. More like a narcissist. Being in bed with the mob does explain some of his odd behavior. It's not like we've got his fingerprints or anything.”

“Yeah. Shit. I was hoping it was him, but I'm thinking we might just have to take him up on his offer for a morning meeting with the mob.”

Sawyer rolled his shoulders, wincing from the motion, then shrugged at Ilse. “See you in the morning, doc. Bright and early. Come strapped.”

He tipped his baseball cap and then turned, strolling back down the hall and whistling to catch the attention of the night sergeant before gesturing back towards the interrogation room.

Ilse sighed, wondering what exactly they'd gotten themselves into.

Bumping heads with the mob was a good way to lose them.

She gave a very Sawyer-esque grumble beneath her breath, then also turned, heading back down the hall towards the exit.

CHAPTER ELEVEN

Ian moved quickly, hands in his pockets, double checking he hadn't dropped any of the tips from today. Oftentimes when sorting receipts and bills, the two could become mixed. Last week, after a double shift, he'd lost half his gratuity.

As he slowed, pausing beneath a streetlamp on the sidewalk, he felt a jolt of relief as his fingers found the rolled up, rubber-banded bills still sitting where he'd left them. He zipped his pocket and continued on his way, whistling as he did.

Tonight had been a good night. A very good night.

He nodded cheerfully as he passed a younger woman walking a very big dog. She had earphones in and didn't acknowledge him. A car zipped by, moving straight through a stop sign.

He watched the vehicle pass, letting out a faint sigh. He wished he had a car of his own. Hell, he wished he had his old job back. Waiting tables was far more stressful than anything he'd done before.

He missed showing up to work, greeted by smiling faces as people lined up, waiting for *his* permission, *his* say-so.

Now, he was the one who had to try and make others happy. Something as simple as bringing the wrong dessert accidentally could cost him his whole tip.

Still...

If he at least had a car, he'd be content.

Another figure was moving in his direction now, down the street, under the watch of the night sky. This man had a dark hood pulled up, the drawstrings tight. He was carrying something in his left hand.

Ian hesitated, feeling a slow prickle down his spine.

He nodded politely as the newcomer approached but also stepped off to the side a bit... one could never be too careful late at night with a wad of bills in one's pocket.

"Got the time?" A voice called from beneath that ominous hood. Both the man's hands were hidden in his sleeves. Definitely not a good sign.

"Sorry man," Ian said. "No watch."

This was a lie. He also had a phone. Mostly, he just wanted to be left alone.

The figure coming towards him... was he moving faster? Shit. Definitely faster. Ian turned, trying to slip between two parked cars.

"Hey man, you dropped this!" the voice behind him said.

Ian's hand automatically went to his zipped pocket. He turned, his heart leaping. The man was holding something out in his left hand... Gripping something tight.

Ian leaned in. "I—that's not mine," he began to say.

Ian's eyes widened as he realized the item was a weapon. He tried to stumble back, but the hooded figure lunged, swinging the weapon and striking Ian across the back of the head with a dull *thwack.*

He stumbled into the hood of one of the parked cars. No screams. No shouts. The woman with the dog was too busy listening to music to notice. The car that had blown the stop sign was long gone.

Ian tried to struggle, tried to push off the hood of the vehicle. Strangely, all he could think of his brother in that moment...

But another blow caught him behind the ear. The pain faded to darkness, and he collapsed between the parked cars with the hooded figure standing over him.

CHAPTER TWELVE

Ilse lay on her bed, staring at the ceiling and willing sleep to visit. She'd managed to get a few hours of sleep here and there but now, glancing at the digital clock next to her bed, it was nearly three AM. Still the dead of night.

She twisted, burying her head beneath her blankets.

But try as she might, she couldn't cut out the dreams. Dark dreams. Haunting dreams. They always seemed to follow her, no matter how far she ran.

The same dreams...

Her father stomping down the stone steps, yelling into the basement to announce his presence. And this time, joined by another figure. A woman in a ghostly dress. A ghoul at her father's back. His accomplice. His lover.

Now they were both shouting at her, both marching down the steps, pursuing her, trying to hunt her down.

Ilse knew she was dreaming. Could even feel the way the blanket wrapped around her ankle. Could feel the way her head burrowed into her pillow. But in a way, this almost made it worse.

As if the nightmares hadn't been content with stealing her subconscious. Now they wanted her while awake as well.

She gritted her teeth, keeping her eyes shut, trying to drown the images. But to no avail.

Her father was laughing now. His accomplice giggled, like a hyena.

And poor little Hilda Mueller ran through the woods. She'd gotten lost. She'd been unable to find her bearings. A neighbor, a hunter, had found her five miles away, nearly frozen to death, her feet cut and bruised. He'd tended to her feet. She hadn't been able to speak at first.

Finally, when she'd managed to get her neighbor to understand her stuttered, terrified words... gotten him to *believe* her, he'd taken her to the authorities. Or, more accurately, he'd waited the weekend for his wife to return. She'd taken Ilse.

Weeks had passed. Weeks where her siblings had suffered horribly.

And all of it could have been avoided if Ilse had simply known where the hell to run to.

“Hilda Mueller,” a voice whispered in her ear. She could feel her father's breath on her cheek. Could feel his fingers against her chin.

She jolted upright, terror sparking through her.

Alone.

Dark.

In bed. She was fine. The tickling on her chin had just been the tag from a pillow. The breath had been a breeze through the slightly cracked window of her apartment.

She blinked, turning to stare at the clock again.

Four AM.

She stared, shaking her head. Such a strange thing to wonder where one's soul went when they slumbered. To lose an hour like that—so quickly?

She shivered, pulling her legs up against herself, wrapping the blankets around her knees. Sweat streamed down her forehead, and yet she was shivering, goose-pimples erupting across her arms.

She looked towards the cracked window, inhaling the breeze shakily.

She missed her old place. Missed the lakeside home, as creepy as it had been at times. Her father had ruined trees and lakes for her too, though, it seemed.

She never could outrun the bastard. And now they wanted to give him another shot at hunting her down.

“Over my dead body,” she muttered. Then, with a sardonic snort, she added, “Most likely.”

She shoved off her bed and moved towards the window, peering out into the night. She pushed the window open a bit further, allowing more breeze to meander through the bedroom. As the breeze wafted over her sweaty features, she noticed faint movement below.

Ilse frowned, peering towards a shadow leaning against the hood of a parked sedan.

A lanky figure sat on the hood of the parked car, staring across the road, his arms crossed. He had leaned back, using the windshield as a sort of bed. His baseball cap was tipped over his face, shielding his eyes. Every so often, the figure shifted again, the shadow moving on the glass.

Ilse blinked, unsure if she was just seeing things. She stared again, but the figure remained.

“Sawyer...” she muttered beneath her breath. She turned back, glancing at the clock again.

Still only 4:13 precisely. It was important to be precise.

She lifted the windowsill but felt a similar unease that she experienced when opening doors, so she closed it, lifted it and closed it again. Then, once her anxiety settled, she pushed the window completely open, leaning her forehead against the mesh screen.

"Psst! Sawyer!" she hissed. She tapped lightly on her own window, staring a couple stories down towards where the laconic agent reclined. "Sawyer!" she said, a bit louder.

He blinked, his eyes like an owl's just visible now beneath his upturned hat. He reached up, pushing the brim back, and stared up at her, still leaning on his car.

Ilse frowned. "What are you doing?" she tried whispering.

Sawyer held a hand to his ear.

"What are you doing out there?" she asked, a bit louder. A light suddenly flashed beneath her—one of the neighbors. Shit. Ilse held up a finger. "Stay there," she called. Then, muttering, "Sorry Mrs. Jenkins," she closed the window, opened, closed it, opened and closed it again.

Then she hastened to get dressed and move towards the front door.

It wasn't like Tom to linger outside her apartment. She supposed he was anxious to get going first thing in the morning, but it wasn't even dawn yet.

She pulled on a light jacket and exited her apartment after her locking ritual. Then, hastily, she took the stairs, anxious to avoid the second-floor landing in case Mrs. Jenkins was peering through the eyehole in order to confront her about the noise.

She reached the apartment door without being accosted and pushed out into the fading night.

Sawyer was now perked up on the hood of his car in the parking lot, his long legs crossed, his hands folded neatly over his knees as if he were simply reclining on a comfortable couch. Ilse slowed, hesitantly approaching Tom.

"Hey," she said cautiously.

"Hey," he said back. Even in the dark, she caught a glint of those familiar green eyes thanks to the light still emanating from Mrs. Jenkins's unit.

Ilse brushed at her hair, wishing she'd had a chance to comb it. No matter—she tugged at her sleeves uncomfortably, twisting on the sidewalk where she stood, half wondering if she ought to just go back inside and get some sleep before trying to deal with whatever *this* was.

"Are you... okay?" she said slowly.

Sawyer shrugged. "Couldn't sleep. Thought we could get a head start."

"Umm... I'm not sure the mobster we're going to meet will be up at this hour."

"Yeah. I guess. Didn't notice the time. My bad."

"So... you've just been sleeping out *on* your car? Why not... you know, *in*."

Sawyer glanced at her, glanced back inside his car towards the comfortable, reclining seat. "Huh," he said. "Good point." He remained where he was.

Ilse let loose a little breath. She paused long enough to glance through the glass door towards her mailbox. No delivery yet. No postcards. Still... it was too early to deal with whatever Sawyer was going through. On the other hand, he clearly needed a listening ear. Emotionally stable people didn't sleep on top of their cars outside co-workers' places of habitation.

Ilse slowly approached, hopping the curb and then patting the black paint. "Can I join you?"

"Yeah... Still probably too early to get Mr. Connolly to—"

"Yeah, Tom. It's definitely too early." Ilse sat on the car slowly, feeling it faintly shift beneath her. The cold metal was uncomfortable against her back. She wasn't sure how long Sawyer had been out here, wasn't sure she *wanted* to know. But then again, she admired his ability to put up with discomfort.

"So," she said carefully. "What's on your mind?"

He glanced at her. "The case."

"Mhmm."

"Really—the case."

"Yup. Definitely."

Sawyer turned a bit now, the car bouncing lightly with the motion. "You got something you wanna say, doc?"

"I don't. But I think you do."

He snorted, turning back again and crossing his arms in an obstinate posture. Ilse did the same. The two of them just stared across the nighttime parking lot, their eyes scanning the motionless cars, the dark windows of the surrounding buildings.

"The stars," he said.

"What?"

"I sat on the roof to see the stars. Kinda hard with all the light pollution, but if you pay attention..." He pointed up, one finger towards the sky. "I don't really know their names."

"Not a stargazer... more of a birdwatcher, right?"

Sawyer smirked. "I still like birds. Like stars too. I named some of them."

"You named them?"

Sawyer shrugged. "I mean, hell, not like officially or anything. But yeah. I named some of them. That one," he said, "I always see it above Seattle. At first I thought it was a satellite. But nope, it's a star."

Ilse followed his pointed finger towards a faint glitter in a dark canvas. "It's nice," she said. "What did you name it?"

Sawyer shot her a look, then glanced back up. He sighed. "Rebekah."

Ilse felt a sudden unexplained surge of emotion at this. His sister's name. Sawyer didn't like talking about his sister, didn't even like mentioning her name. Sometimes, Ilse thought even *thinking* about her caused him pain.

Sawyer shrugged. "I'm sure it's probably got a real name. Maybe part of the Big Dipper or something."

Ilse hid a smile. "You can't see the Big Dipper tonight."

"Oh, well... you know. To me that's always been Bekah. Sometimes I just like seeing it. In a city, most stars are hidden from all the lights. Drowns them out. Hides them. But that one—that one right there—is always visible."

"Yeah..." Ilse said, still feeling that same, strange emotion. Her chest prickling with compassion. Part of her wanted to reach out, to hug him. To tell him it was all going to be okay. Another part of her just wanted to cry. She could feel the pain in her partner coming off in waves. Could practically taste the agony on the air with every word.

Sawyer didn't cry. Didn't much speak about those sorts of things.

He allowed the wounds to fester. Insisted on tending to them himself.

In all her life, Ilse had never seen someone heal on their own. People were communal. People needed each other—needed help. She wished, somehow, she could get Sawyer to believe that too.

She opened her mouth to say something, but Sawyer continued, in a far quieter, whisper of a voice. "I once heard a lot of those stars are dead. You see their light because they're millions of light years away. But they've been dead for a long time."

Ilse felt a lump in her throat. She closed her mouth, not speaking at all. She reached out faintly and patted Sawyer on the wrist in what she hoped was a comforting gesture.

He didn't withdraw. Didn't say anything.

The two of them just sat there, Ilse's fingers resting against Sawyer's wrist. Both of them experiencing their own type of pain. Different forms of grief.

And that's when Sawyer's phone began to ring.

He moved swiftly, reaching into his pocket. Ilse noticed, though, that he left the hand she was touching unmoved, as if not wanting to disturb her. With his other hand, though, he put the phone to his ear.

"Yeah?" Sawyer said, a bit more eagerly than Ilse felt this early in the morning.

Ilse stared at the side of her partner's face, waiting, listening.

"Mhmm," Sawyer said. "Got it. Er, yeah... Yeah I'll call her. No, sir. That's fine—I'm sure she'll pick up." He shot her a quick wink. "Alright, heading there now. No—no don't you let them move the body, Rawley. Dammit, don't move it. We're coming!"

He hung up.

Ilse let out a faint, shaking breath. "Another one?" she whispered.

Sawyer was slipping off the car now, finally retracting his hand. "Third body was found in another scrapyard." He moved towards the door, swinging it open.

Ilse felt a faint numbness creeping across her skin. Sawyer's closure rate was one thing. But the *people* dying would easily have been the sorts she'd invite, open-armed into her office. The sorts she would counsel. And now someone was killing them left and right. She felt queasy but forced herself to focus on the case. There was only one way to stop this. "I guess that clears Mr. Connolly. He's been in jail."

Sawyer looked across the top of the car, scowling. He sighed but nodded. "Guess so. Come on, doc—they're holding the body for us." His eyes narrowed, and something darker, more dangerous than she was accustomed to finding in those green windows, suddenly displayed. "He's getting away with it. We have to get this guy. Crush him."

With those ominous words, Sawyer slipped into the driver's seat, gesturing for Ilse to join him passenger-side.

CHAPTER THIRTEEN

Dawn crested as they pulled towards large metal gates outside this new scrapyard. Ilse stared through the window, listening as Sawyer got off the phone. “You're sure?” Tom was saying, driving with one hand, gripping his phone with the other in a way that made Ilse uncomfortable every time Sawyer had merged.

“Yeah... Yeah that's fine, keep him—take a statement. But cut him loose. Yeh—right now.” He hung up. At the same time, he pulled the car to a halt.

Ilse stared. “What was that?”

Sawyer shook his head. “Got word back on that little group of organized criminals Mr. Connolly was talking about.”

“Yeah?”

Sawyer snorted, practically kicking open his door facing the metal gate. “It ain't the mob. Just a bunch of low-level radio thieves. They're not killers—they're teenagers with daddy issues.”

Ilse winced. “I mean, I guess that confirms they weren't involved. Especially since this scrapyard looks pretty well protected.” She nodded through the window towards the large, barbed-wire fence.

Unlike the last scrapyard, this one—nearly twenty miles from the city—had two rings of metal blockade surrounding it. The wire was thick. The barbed wire doubled up and fastened securely on top. No cameras that Ilse could see, but a couple of signs warned about dogs on the premises.

In the background, Ilse thought she heard barking.

“Radio-thieves aren't exactly what we're looking for,” Sawyer said. “What with this new body, I told them to cut Connolly loose.”

Ilse nodded. This made sense to her also. Still, this early, with sunlight only just now rising, she tried to hold back a wide yawn but failed. With a resigned sigh, she pushed open her door and joined Sawyer on a surprisingly well-kept, black asphalt road. It looked as if it had been recently poured in the last month or so.

She shivered at the thought of a third victim. Images of the last two flashed through her mind's eye. What sort of grisly display would meet them now?

She winced at the thought, tugging uncomfortably at her sweater sleeves and following after Sawyer as he approached the metal gate.

A man was sitting in a white booth—which seemed to serve as a functional guard house. As the two of them strolled up, he waved them down. He stuck his head out the window, thin strands of downy brown hair fluttering thanks to a window fan.

"Can I help you?" the man called.

"Where are the cops?" Sawyer returned.

The man jammed a finger over his shoulder. "Waiting for the feds. You them?"

Sawyer nodded. He wiggled his hand towards the door. "Open up please."

But the man in the guardhouse said, "Got ID?"

Sawyer didn't bother, but Ilse flashed hers and the man called, over the sound of his window fan, "One sec." He reached into his guardhouse and pushed a button on the wall. A second later, the gate rattled and began to open.

With the barbed wire, the automatic gate, the mention of cops, feds and ID, Ilse almost felt like they were entering a prison.

She noticed Sawyer staring at the gate, glancing towards the guardhouse, frowning.

She nudged him. "You okay?"

He blinked, startled from his reverie. "I—what? Yeah. Fine, fine. Come on, cops are holding the body. Coroner was pissed half an hour ago with Rawley. No sense getting the big man more flak."

He jammed his hands into his jeans pockets, nodded towards the gate guard and moved through the open door up the newly poured black asphalt path. Ilse stared after him, frowned towards the gate, the barbed wire, then gave a sigh and faint shake of her head as she followed after him towards a crime scene that she knew she didn't want to see.

As they moved, Ilse was impressed at how much more *clean* this particular metal-processing yard was. The cars, the appliances, old containers, and scrap metal were all sorted, locked behind gates. Nothing was piled so high that it threatened to topple. Everything had signs, labels, and estimated weight. She heard the sound of barking and spotted a couple of Dobermans behind a gate with a sign that read, "Copper wire."

As they moved along the new road, ahead, she spotted a far prettier office. A two-story, white-painted structure with violet trim. It had a garage on one wing, with the gray doors opened and a couple of cars on lifts.

Sawyer pointed. “Guess it was early to get too many guys out.”

Ilse spotted a different road, looking as if it came from the opposite direction of the scrapyard. Parked on the side of this path, inside the gates, she spotted two police cars and a dormant ambulance.

One cop was sitting inside a car, sipping a coffee. Another was standing in the middle of the pathway talking to an overweight fellow in a lab coat that exposed a sliver of his belly. This man was gesticulating wildly, pointing at the sun, then down the road.

The cop held out a hand in what looked like a placating gesture and was saying something Ilse couldn't quite hear.

“Rawley wasn't lying,” Sawyer said with a snort. “Coroner is *pissed.* Guy ain't local neither.”

Ilse sighed. Just what she needed first thing in the morning—getting yelled at.

“Hey y'all,” Sawyer said, raising a hand.

The arguing coroner and cop paused, turning to frown at the newcomers.

“Can we help you?” the cop asked.

Tom said, “Agent Sawyer. This is Doctor Beck. The body still displayed?”

The cop relaxed a bit, seeming almost relieved. The man took a few steps away, putting distance between him and the irate coroner. The second man, though, turned, redirecting his scowl towards Sawyer.

“Are you the cretin who stopped me from taking the body?” Ilse winced as a chubby finger jutted skyward, and began to whip around, like a conductor's baton.

"Calm down," Sawyer said. "We just needed to see it. Look, hang on. *Quiet!*"

The coroner had been speaking, louder and louder, trying to cut Sawyer off. At this final declaration, though, the big man went still, his lips pressed into a tight, thin line. He gave a long exhalation of frustration and said, "If you don't want me to do my job. I won't do my job."

And then, summoning the residue of his dignity, he marched off, stiff-legged, pulling at his trousers which threatened to slip.

Ilse flinched as the irate coroner stopped past her, but then joined Sawyer on the road, moving towards where the third victim had been found. They didn't need a signpost. They didn't need directions.

Ilse felt drawn to it, like a moth to flame. She took hesitant, stumbling steps forward, her eyes the size of saucers.

She let out a shaking, shuttering exhalation.

"Don't worry about the coroner," Sawyer muttered. "He'll be back when we need him."

But Ilse wasn't even paying attention. She was staring towards the horrible display.

A figure had been dismembered. Parts of the body were welded with metal rings to what looked like railroad ties. Though they were a bit too small. Tracks?

Ilse looked at the horrible spectacle set inside one of the mesh-link fences. No dogs growled over here. The employees kept their distance.

No barbed wire topped this particular metal container either. But inside, Ilse spotted the abdomen. The legs had been removed and wrapped around the tracks. The metal tracks themselves were shaped like a DNA strand, jutting straight up out of the ground. Someone had gone to great lengths to place this pillar of twisting metal in the middle of the cage. They had gone to similar lengths to slot body parts in a grotesque fashion, through premade metal rings.

It was bizarre. Grotesque. The eye didn't quite know where to land. Ilse found herself hyperventilating, standing there, but wishing desperately she was anywhere else.

"How did they ID him?" Ilse said with a shudder.

Sawyer muttered, "The head. It's in that basket over there. Tried to get prints, but the right hand is missing. Left hand is burned."

Ilse didn't look. She couldn't bring herself to it. She decided to trust Sawyer on his word alone. Her stomach was doing flips as she stared away from the horrible spectacle. “The right hand is missing?” she murmured.

“That's what the cops wrote in initial findings.” Sawyer shrugged.

Part of her wanted to turn and scream. A part of her was also caught in place with grim fascination.

A sadist. She'd called it at the start. Someone obsessed with power, inflicting pain, but also fear.

The spectacle alone, intent on drawing the eye, was clearly the work of a narcissist. The combination of the two traits suggested antisocial personality disorder. Suggested the killer wouldn't feel one ounce of remorse for what he was doing.

Ilse shivered, rubbing at her arms. "What does it even mean?"

Sawyer shook his head, still staring at the grisly presentation, while

Ilse preferred to watch him. "Hydraulic press with the first victim. A totaled car with the second. And now a weird train tracks statue."

"I don't think the tracks are big enough for a train."

Sawyer just shook his head. "The first two weren't dismembered like this."

"It's awful."

"Any other gleanings, doc?"

Ilse tugged nervously at the sleeves of her sweater. She considered the question, paused, cycling through what she knew about killers who dismembered their victims.

"The last two cases the corners didn't find any sign of sexual assault. No necrophilia."

This time it was Sawyer's turn to wrinkle his nose.

Ilse pressed on. "No cannibalism. The butchery isn't meant for him, it's meant for us. It also," she said, faintly, "could be meant for the victims."

"What does that mean?" Sawyer said.

Ilse frowned, and slowly began to answer, but as she opened her mouth, a sudden scream split the air.

Ilse and Sawyer whirled about, staring in the direction of the office.

A rusty blue truck had just pulled up. It was parked askew over two spots. A man in overalls, wearing workers gloves, and displaying a wild, unkempt head of hair was staring in their direction.

Another worker was standing next to him, restraining him. One hand clasped on his shoulder, where he was muttering something. Ilse noticed the worker could only comfort with a single hand because he only *had* one hand. The other was conspicuously missing, cut at the forearm.

But whatever comforting words the one-armed man was trying to convey were lost on the fellow who had just emerged from the blue truck. The wild-haired man in overalls stumbled forward, screaming again. "Ian!" he yelled. His voice groaned with agony.

He tried to take another tottering step towards the crime scene, sobbing horribly, his shoulders shaking.

"Who is that?" Sawyer barked, pointing towards the junkyard worker.

"His brother," the man replied. “We know him around here—sometimes does work for us.”

Sawyer cursed. "The brother?"

Ilse held out a hand towards the distressed individual. "Sir, you don't want to see this. Please stay back."

"What did they do to Ian!" sobbed the man in overalls. His voice shook horribly, his face lost its blood. He stumbled to his knees, hitting the dust, and slumping over. He continued to shake. His friend reached down, trying to keep a hand on his shoulder in a comforting gesture but the effort was futile.

"This can't be happening," the victim's brother was saying. "Dear God. How is this happening?"

Ilse was hurrying forward. Sawyer was scowling at the second worker. "Why is the victim's brother here?"

The one-handed worker shook his head. "Guy in the guardhouse called him—they've been buds since school."

Sawyer cursed again, walking in a straight line as if trying to block the view of the crime scene behind them.

The second worker was trying to lead the victim's brother away, trying to drag him back towards the clean office building.

"Please," Ilse said, joining them, "you don't want to be here. Let's go inside. We can have some coffee."

"I don't want coffee. What happened? Are you sure he's dead?"

Ilse winced, picturing the horrible scene within the metal cage. "Look, why don't you calm down. You can help answer some questions."

Right now, the only way to console the man was to distract him from his grief. Questions had a way of eliciting that. It was often suggested, for instance, if you were about to get mugged, to ask the attacker what time it was. Even though they were entirely focused on stealing your money or phone or wallet, their knee-jerk reaction to that question would fire a part of the brain automatically. On pure instinct. Sometimes, this even gave the victim a chance to escape their mugger.

Similarly, in her practice, questions were often used to reengage certain parts of the brain.

"Is that your favorite color?" Ilse said, pointing at his shirt.

She just needed him to hear, to process the question. She didn't need an answer. As he blinked in confusion, and glanced down at his outfit, Ilse tugged at his arm. "How about we head inside."

Sniffing, shaking, he allowed himself to be pulled to his feet.

He hadn't seen the body. But the sight of the two FBI agents had been enough to set him off. The cops further back were both watching with concern etched across their expressions. The early morning sunlight did little to warm the scene.

The man leaned against his friend but couldn't be bothered to take another step towards the office.

His voice warbled. "Ian didn't deserve this. He was trying his best! After all that shit last year at the fair, we were settling in. It is not fair. It is not fair!"

Ilse tried to track this. Two uses of the word fair. She said, "What business last year?"

But the man shook his head. "He was gonna buy a new guitar—try to get back into music."

Ilse waited patiently for this new wave of sobbing to subside. Sawyer had turned and marched back towards the ghoulish diorama, examining the scene further. Ilse preferred to stand next to the living. She said, "Sir, please, for your brother's sake, help me. What did you mean about last year?"

Again, he couldn't seem to hear the question.

So Ilse tried something about his brother. This was who was occupying his mind. "Was your brother a conductor at one point? Did he like trains?"

He finally looked up, sniffing. He stared out at her from under his wild fringe. "What?"

Ilse just shook her head. "Not trains then?"

"I don't think he knew much about trains. Why?"

Ilse just shook her head. At least he was engaging now. But if he wasn't interested in trains, what with the point of the tracks melded together, used to present the body?

She tried a third time to get him to focus on the comment he'd made earlier. "You said something happened last year," she said softly. "What were you talking about?"

They had moved a few feet closer, as they spoke, towards the large office building, mostly due to the insistent tugs of the second worker.

But now, standing on the new asphalt, in the shadow of the building, the man just looked at her, and an expression of bitterness took his face. "It wasn't fair. Wasn't fair at all. Ask anyone. They did wrong by us. My brother did the best he could. It was a shit job. He didn't have all the time he needed to check everything."

"I'm sorry, but please help me. What job?"

The man jammed his thumb through his overall straps, tears still streaking his face, his eyes red and puffy. He looked off towards the office building and grumbled. "It was this stupid local fair. They had some rides. We both worked there. We liked working together..."

"I can see that," Ilse said, her tone energetic, encouraging. Interested. "And something happened at this fair?"

"Yeah. It wasn't Ian's fault. There was an accident with one of the rides. A roller coaster."

Ilse blinked, forcing herself to focus, refusing to turn and glanced back towards the welded tracks. "Alright, a roller coaster. Were people injured?"

"Yeah. A couple. It was bad."

Ilse said, "How bad?"

"Sue the city bad. But it wasn't my brother's fault. He checked everything. He always did. At least, he did his best. But we were running low on crew. He was trying to operate three different rides. It wasn't fair. They didn't hire enough operators."

Ilse nodded sympathetically. She patted the man on his shoulder. "I'm very sorry."

The man cut in, "It was just a stupid amusement park. They could've paid a high school kid to help out. Saved everyone a huge headache. Save my brother his job. And now this."

Again, he pointed past her and began to shake.

Ilse went quiet, allowing him to experience the grief uninterrupted. Her heart went out to him. She wanted to sit him down, to talk to him. To help him.

The same way she wanted to help Sawyer.

But she couldn't help everyone. And right now, people were dying. She needed to focus.

She gave a sympathetic look towards the man, then double-checked to make sure his friend was still there, and she turned, moving back towards Sawyer.

As she walked, her expression flickered, morphing into a frown.

Was he telling the truth?

This third victim had nothing to do with an amusement park accident that caused injuries enough to sue the city?

Ilse shivered, feeling goosebumps across her skin.

And what was that Mr. Wagonmaker had said about his son Matthew? He had gotten into an accident recently too. No one had been hurt... allegedly. But maybe it was time to verify that claim. She picked up her pace, hastening towards Tom to tell him what she'd found.

CHAPTER FOURTEEN

Ilse sat in the back seat of their car, in the parking lot outside the junkyard. They were motionless, sitting on the asphalt with their windows cracked. The sun was still low in the sky, slowly rising to meet a new day. Ilse had moved into the backseat, in order to focus. Sawyer was chatting on his phone, his voice rising in volume with each passing moment. She caught scattered words of the conversation. "What do you mean you *don't know*? He worked for you just a few weeks ago... You better have records."

Ilse strived to focus on her own task, though. While her recalcitrant partner hunted down leads on the other two victims, she was digging into the second victim.

Matthew Wagonmaker. Luckily, as with most major vehicle accidents, there was a police report.

She sat with Sawyer's laptop open in front of her. She didn't own a mobile computer of her own and Sawyer had long ago given up on trying to make her purchase one. Now, it was mostly a matter of habit that she borrowed his.

And while he continued to browbeat someone over the phone in the background, Ilse tried to focus on the article in front of her.

Both a police report, and an online news article confirmed the same thing.

Matthew had been in a car crash. He'd accidentally turned the wrong way onto a highway and had been going in the wrong direction before careening into another vehicle.

Matthew, only a teenager, had gotten away unharmed, though his car had been totaled. The passengers in the other vehicle, though, hadn't been nearly so lucky.

Ilse leaned in, her fingers touching the smooth glass of the computer. She read and re-read the article. She then moved to the browser and looked at the police report again.

They both confirmed the same thing.

One of the passengers in the other vehicle had died. Hadn't been wearing a seatbelt.

It was based on this technicality that Matthew hadn't been given prison time. Everything had been declared an accident. No drugs or drink in his system. Though, Ilse couldn't help but notice that the officer who'd written the report, hadn't thought to breathalyze the young man.

It wasn't until a day later, that they checked his blood alcohol content for formality's sake.

Their second victim had gotten away free. Nothing on his record, nothing legally. The people in the other car had lost a woman on the passenger side. Another person had been injured.

Ilse confirmed what she'd read once more, and then slowly, with a strong sense of distaste, lowered her laptop screen and waited for a lull in Sawyer's most recent tirade.

He was saying, "Yes, I've read the lawsuit. I want to hear it from *you*. Was there negligence or not?" Sawyer paused, waiting. And then he cursed. He lowered his phone, and turned back, staring at Ilse. "They hung up."

"Shocking," said Ilse.

Sawyer shook his head, muttering darkly beneath his breath. After a moment, he looked back again. His green eyes flashed. "Did you find anything?"

"I think I did actually. I checked the police report on that accident that the second victim's father mentioned."

Sawyer nodded.

"The father said no one was hurt I think, but maybe I'm misremembering."

"No. He said that."

"Well, he was either mistaken or lying. His son killed someone."

Sawyer's expression darkened into a scowl.

"What about you?"

Sawyer shook his head. "Two calls. The first one, the shift manager at that factory near where the first victim was found said that she was actually involved in an accident with one of the machines. Apparently, she didn't inspect it properly and another coworker was crushed."

Ilse blinked in surprise. "Well then."

"I couldn't get the carnival manager to say much. Or whatever, an amusement park. I don't really know the difference. But anyway, it sounded like it was possible that our third victim was negligent on the job. Didn't follow basic safety instructions."

"His brother seemed adamant, even with him dead, that it wasn't his fault."

Sawyer nodded. "That would probably be because of the liability from the lawsuit. The amusement park had to shell out millions. It nearly closed them down."

"I guess it makes sense why they fired him."

The two agents went quiet, sitting in the car, motionless.

"Well," Ilse said.

"Well," Sawyer repeated.

"What do you think it means?"

"I'm more of a paint by number type of guy, doc. This was your lead. I've got my theory. What's yours?"

She paused for a moment, exhaling, then said, "The first victim was caught in a hydraulic press. The second victim was found in a totaled car. The third victim was found with scattered pieces of their body stapled to train tracks."

"Too small for train tracks," Sawyer said, lobbing back her own comment from earlier.

"Maybe roller coaster tracks," Ilse said.

Sawyer tapped his nose and pointed at her.

Ilse sighed. "So that has to be the connection, right?"

"You think our psycho sadist is going after people who survived accidents?"

"Who *caused* accidents. And then also survived unscathed. But the other people involved in the accidents were either hurt or killed."

"I mean, it makes sense. Perfect sense. But only one thing."

"What's that?"

"How the hell does that help us *find the guy*?"

Silence descended on the vehicle once more. The two of them sat, considering their options. Ilse felt a jolt of grief. So many accidents, so many damaged people. Some of them dead, others injured, and still others maimed for life.

She thought back to the epiphany she'd had at the third crime scene. What if this wasn't about the killer but about his victims. He was full of anger, that much was clear. Did he see himself as some sort of agent of justice? Was he a vigilante?

Did he know about all these cases of people escaping unharmed from accidents they'd caused?

How was he even finding them? How was he targeting them? The local news?

It seemed difficult. Some of the cases went back a few years. The killer would've had to be very careful. Unless he had been planning this for years.

Ilse shook her head. "We still need to find a suspect. We know why but still don't know who, or even how. They have to be a metalworker or a welder. Someone in the trades."

"Maybe. Or else they hired someone without telling them what they were going to use the horrible contraptions for."

Ilse shook her head in frustration. "No cameras in any of the scrapyards. He's coming in at night. That's obvious."

"It has to be night. Someone would notice during the day."

"You think he has a truck? To carry such heavy machinery, there has to be a vehicle larger than just some stupid sedan."

Sawyer hesitated, tapping his chin. "Smart, doc. It has to be a big vehicle. Maybe he has a trailer. Or maybe he's driving a semi or a flatbed."

"But if it's something that big, surely someone at the scrapyard would've noticed."

"I wouldn't be so sure. These places are super understaffed after hours."

Ilse let out a huff of air. "Alright, so let's go with that. He's driving some big vehicle, getting in late at night, and going to scrapyards without any cameras to record him."

"The office actually back there had a camera."

"I saw it. No wires. No batteries. And it was facing the office door."

Sawyer grunted.

Ilse hesitated, then said, "All three of the victims have been found in three different scrapyards, different locations. Maybe that's the angle to narrow down how he's dumping them. What if he is familiar with his grounds?"

Sawyer's eyebrows shot up. "You think he works for these places? I'm not sure they share employees. From what I gathered it was pretty much a 9-to-5 type of gig"

"Don't forget the late shifts. But yes, it's full-time. But what if, seeing as we've been talking about trucks, what if it's one of the people that dumps all this material. It's not like the workers go out and collect the trucks, the cars, the appliances, and the scraps. People dump this stuff. Do you think maybe there's someone associated with all three locations?"

Sawyer considered this for a moment, and then snapped his fingers. "You know what, I was talking to one of the employees back at the crime scene, and he mentioned how they actually use something like a distribution service. They hire contractors to go through with local recycling companies and parse out any of the useful material; then these contractors drop off the profitable material at the scrapyards, to be reused or resold, or repurposed.

Ilse clicked her fingers. "Is there a way we can see who these contractors are? Cross-reference their names?

"I've actually got you one better."

Ilse watched as Sawyer raised his phone, cycled through his numbers, scrolling to the bottom.

"Who are you calling?"

"Me and Gabriel hit it off."

Ilse waited for him to fill in the blanks, but he didn't. "Who is Gabriel?"

He glanced at her. "The guy who let us into the third junkyard." He nodded ahead, through the windshield up the hill towards the office. "While you were consoling the grieving brother and his friend, Gabriel and I had a chat. He's the one who mentioned contractors."

Ilse waited as the phone connected. Sawyer allowed it to go to video.

The two of them sat in the car, watching the screen vibrate. And then, a few seconds later, a face appeared in the image.

A man was sitting in what looked to be a well air-conditioned room, sipping a beer.

"What's up Tom dog!" said Gabriel. He smirked and raised his beer in greeting.

"How's it going, Gabe," Sawyer said. "Just calling to thank you for all your help today."

"No problem, man. Did you have any more questions about barbed wire?"

"No," Sawyer said, a bit too quickly. "That's fine. The barbed wire's a no go. Nothing to do with the case. We think the killer came in by truck."

Ilse frowned, watching Sawyer. She glanced through the windshield again at the barbed wire circling the third crime scene. The junkyard was an ominous thing from the outside.

Why had Sawyer been asking about barbed wire? Most likely just tracking a lead that didn't turn out. It was obvious the killer couldn't come in over the fence. Not possible with the machinery he had to bring in with him.

Sawyer seemed eager to move past this line of questioning, and was hurriedly saying, "Look, just wondering, do you have a way we can check those contractors you were mentioning? The truck drivers who drop off material."

"Yeah. I got the company name. They can give you route information. Employee information. There are a few companies that do all this. But in our region, there's only one big one."

"Yeah, let's start with the big one. Give me the rest just in case."

"Well, for us, it's only the big one. The small one quit five years ago."

Ilse leaned in, waving over the seat. "Hello Gabriel. This is Dr. Beck. Just send us the main company, please."

"You got it. Take care, Tom dog." He hung up. A second later, Tom's phone vibrated, and the screen displayed a blue hyperlink.

Industrial Distribution. Ilse read the name of the company over Sawyer's shoulder. He clicked the link, and it took them to a website. The site looked old, the pictures of the trucks on the front also outdated. But there was a phone number available.

"Think we should call or go in person?" Sawyer asked.

"I'm thinking maybe we should contact Rudiger," Ilse said slowly.

Sawyer let out a faint sigh.

Ilse winced and shrugged apologetically. "You know how those guys can be. If we start asking for employee records, or cross-referencing drivers between the different scrapyards, they're going to put up a lot of red tape; on the other hand, Rudiger has never failed to get us a list yet. Remember with those community centers?"

Sawyer was shaking his head. He pushed open the door to the car, stepping out onto the sidewalk. Ilse pushed out the back, joining him where he stretched, rubbing at his neck.

"Oh come on, I know you like the guy. Stop pretending you don't," Ilse said. "Besides, it could help speed things up." Her heart skipped at the thought of this. The killer was murdering at a rapid rate. They didn't have time to get a warrant. Didn't have time for bureaucrats. They needed those names, needed to start checking boxes.

Sawyer began to stroll around the car, circling it, like the moon around the earth. "For the record I *tolerate* the guy. I like him on occasion. *Rare* occasions. Mostly he's annoying."

"Sure."

"Fine. Just let the record show this was your idea, doc."

She held her hand up solemnly and placed it over her heart. Sawyer lifted his phone again, this time refusing to go to video chat, and he scrolled down. He dialed a number and waited.

Not even a full ring completed. After half a ring, an energetic, flamboyant voice boomed over the speaker.

"Tommy, darling! Absolutely spiffing to hear from you. How are you? I've been missing you so much. But such is the life of a roaming bachelor. I'm sure you understand."

Ilse blinked in the face of this wordy introduction.

Sawyer just scratched his chin, looked at the phone, then hung up.

"Tom!" Ilse protested, scandalized.

Sawyer grumbled, but muttered, "Fine, fine." He dialed the number again.

Rudiger, completely unperturbed, declared, "Looks like I lost you there for a second, Tommy boy. What can I do for you? Anything from Uncle Rudy. Say, is that pretty little thing still with you?"

"Hello Rudy," Ilse said, cheerfully. The aureate, Hawaiian shirt-wearing tech agent didn't bother her nearly as much as he did Sawyer.

"Ilse," he said, a trill to his voice. "Marvelous. Wonderful. You sound as lovely as I remember. How is Tom doing? Is he still wearing that awful hat?"

Ilse winced, glancing at Sawyer, and back at the phone. She cleared her throat while Tom massaged the bridge of his nose. "Rudiger, we actually have a favor to ask. Do you have time?"

"For you, dear, anything. And more. I recently got involved with this backroom blackjack table. It's been going well. So if you hear me clicking away while we chat, don't mind it."

Sawyer muttered, "He's probably playing video games."

"I heard that, Tommy!"

"You were meant to, Rudy. Look, we need you to check out a website. It's outdated, and I can't imagine the encryption is strong. We need to know the schedules of truckers."

"Trucker schedules. Great. Why can't it ever be hookers? Dope fiends. Assassins. Something interesting. Something difficult. What's the website? Actually, no, never mind. I think I found it here on your phone. It's the one with the link, right? The industry professionals?"

Sawyer growled. "Rudiger, how do you see my phone?"

Rudy didn't even answer; he just gave a giggling little laugh. "Tommy, dear, don't fret yourself. Let's see what I can find for you."

Sawyer was busy cycling through the apps on his phone, making sure there was nothing watching his activity. Ilse was grateful she'd never purchased a smart phone. The two of them stood in the parking lot outside the barbed wire fence, waiting.

It didn't take long for Rudiger to declare, "What am I looking for exactly?"

"Anyone who has a route that includes the three scrapyards from the most recent case file. Case 1025."

"1025? Got it. Yuck. Look at these. Someone's been busy with a hacksaw."

Ilse wrinkled her nose. Sawyer just sighed again. Rudy began whistling a friendly tune, and it took Ilse a second to realize it was a Christmas carol.

Rudy paused long enough to swallow something. She remembered the large bowl of jellybeans he kept by his computer. After a moment, though, the energetic coder said, "Some of these guys share routes. But from what I see, they actually only hire three truckers."

Sawyer suddenly perked up in interest. "Three?"

"It's a big number. I can count to it for you, if you like."

"Rudy, if you weren't so useful, I might reveal that you weren't as charming as you thought you were."

Rudiger scoffed. "Don't mind him, Ilse. Sometimes he says things when he's hungry. I know he doesn't mean it. But Sawyer, Tom, look, of the three names, only one of them frequently visits the locations you sent me. All of them visit the locations on occasion. But only this one driver visits all three."

"I'm not sure that made sense."

Rudiger sighed. "Only one driver visits all three regularly. Do you want his name or not?" Rudiger gave a little click of his tongue. "In fact, would you look at that, he's on a route right now. If you start moving, you can reach him in twenty minutes."

Sawyer scowled. "How do you know where we are?"

"Tommy, let me help you. Ready? I'm sending you his information. His driver's license photo. A screenshot of his last journal entry. And here are some images I think his girlfriend may have sent him. On second thought, those last ones are just for me. Have a good day. Ta-ta!"

Rudiger hung up. Sawyer's phone buzzed again. And again. And again. And then it started ringing with the same Christmas carol Rudiger had been whistling.

It took Sawyer nearly a minute to figure out how to shut off the sound.

Grumbling, he shoved back into the car. Ilse, quiet, slipped into the front seat.

"We never should've called him," Sawyer said.

"It was helpful," Ilse replied, "wasn't it?"

"That's not the point. It's the principle of the matter. Whatever, the guy, the trucker, Amos Reck."

"His last name is Reck?"

Sawyer shrugged. "I didn't name him. Rudy is right. He's driving a semi to a junkyard twenty minutes from here. Think we should meet him en route?"

Ilse nodded. "He was connected to all three crime scenes? Connected to the scrapyards. And he drives a semi-truck. The perfect way to haul a hydraulic press, totaled car, and even that train track piece."

"Shit. If you think about it, employees might not even notice those trucks. Might not think it's worth mentioning. Stuff like that has a way of fading into the background."

Ilse nodded. She could feel her excitement mounting. "Let's go talk to Mr. Reck and see if he knows anything."

CHAPTER FIFTEEN

Ilse pointed out the window as traffic slowed to a crawl on the highway. The wind against her cheeks faded as their speed declined.

The source of the embargo was clear enough: a curling offramp with a thin shoulder had a line of cars backed up. One by one, occasionally leaning on their horns, they maneuvered around a large truck, with a towing hook on the back. The truck was about half the size of a cargo vehicle. Three rusted, dilapidated vehicles sat on a flat metal bed. But a fourth vehicle, mostly rust and neglect, looked to have fallen half in the road.

A man with a scraggly beard, a baseball cap, and a grease-stained shirt was hastily trying to hook this rusted jalopy to a winch and crank it back onto his flatbed.

But as he did, he blocked half the second lane of traffic. Another car slipped by, leaning on its horn.

"Think that's our guy?" Ilse asked, still pointing. "That's our exit, isn't it?"

Sawyer pulled closer, frowning, and peering through the windshield towards the license plate.

The numbers were mostly blocked as the mechanic tried to place a metal hook beneath the hood of the car. The man moved around, jolting every time one of the drivers leaned on his horn.

A Mercedes convertible slipped around the edge of the rusty bumper, honking, and the driver shouting, "Moron!"

The mechanic cursed, flinging a wrench at the back of the fleeing vehicle. A taillight shattered. Red glass scattered. The Mercedes slammed on its brakes. It began to try and back up.

The mechanic turned, pulling to his full height. "Get out then!" the man bellowed.

Sawyer waited his turn, patiently jammed behind a minivan full of kids who were watching the spectacle in awe from behind their windows, as if they were at a zoo. Ilse tapped her leg nervously as they inched forward.

Sawyer's hand was on the door, as if preparing to jump out in case he was needed.

Thankfully, the Mercedes driver flashed another middle finger, echoed a series of expletives, and then drove off again without further altercation.

The mechanic, indifferent to the cars around him, stomped across the road, grabbed his wrench, and then stomped back. Only then allowing the minivan to pull around him.

The flash of angry brake lights cleared, allowing Sawyer and Ilse to access the shoulder on the curve.

Sawyer pulled over, behind the large vehicle with the junked cars.

"Industrial Distribution," Sawyer muttered, nodding towards the gray lettering on the front of the cabin.

Ilse noticed this as well and nodded. She kept her eyes on the mechanic, who had finally managed to hook the front bumper, and was now applying pressure to the winch. The chain went taut, and the front of the car began to lift; the front wheels landed on the back strip of the truck, and the mechanic tried to adjust its trajectory.

"It doesn't look like he's in a very good mood," Ilse murmured.

They exited the car, slamming the doors behind them.

"Mr. Reck?" Sawyer called out.

Any remaining doubt as to the identity of the mechanic ended when the man perked and turned at the name.

His expression was dour, his eyebrows low, his eyes narrowed. Ilse detected the faint hint of gasoline lingering on the air. The heat from the exhaust pipe in front of them wafted over her face, and she wrinkled her nose, trying not to breathe in too deeply.

Now that the rusted car had been lifted on its front tires, the road was cleared again. Traffic began to pick up its pace. The honking, mercifully, subsided.

"Amos Reck?" Sawyer repeated.

"Who's asking?"

"FBI," Sawyer returned. "Agent Sawyer. This is Dr. Beck. We'd like to ask you a few questions."

The moment Sawyer announced himself as a law enforcement official, Reck tensed. His hand flinched, and the wrench he'd thrown earlier clattered to the ground. His eyes were dilated, and he swallowed, a pronounced Adam's apple rising and falling. He reached out, smoothing his scraggly beard as if to make himself more presentable. At the same time, he wiped his hands off on his already grease-stained shirt.

"Don't mind her," Sawyer said suddenly, as Ilse edged further away from the traffic and stood near the concrete barrier. Reck kept looking at her uncomfortably. "What type of doctor?" he said.

Ilse wrinkled her nose. A strange question. "Trauma psychologist," she said.

He looked disappointed. He sighed, shaking his head. "You write prescriptions too?"

"You need one?" she said.

Sawyer seemed to decide that the truck-driver was no threat for the moment. Like this, he passed the baton to her to continue the conversation, while he slowly moved around the edge of the truck, glancing through gaps in the rusted vehicles.

Instead of continuing to talk with Ilse, though, the mechanic looked over. "What are you doing?"

"Just looking," Sawyer said.

Ilse cleared her throat, trying to regain his attention. "Sir, I'd like to ask you a few things if you don't mind."

He snorted. "I have a choice?"

"It's not like that. Not yet. We just want to know if you've been adhering to your route recently. Where are you coming from right now?"

He shrugged. "Scrapyard. That a crime?" He fiddled with one of the brass buttons on his shirt then glanced toward Sawyer who was now leaning into the cabin of the truck, peering inside.

"Hey," he called out. "You can't do that!"

Ilse and Sawyer both perked up at his tone. Fear. Sweat trickled along his upper lip. His eyes were red, bloodshot. He looked nervous, sleepless. His foot was tapping against the ground.

Ilse's hand slowly strayed towards her holster. She rested her fingers against the leather. "Sir, did you get much sleep last night?"

He shot her a shifty look. He wet his lips with a pale tongue. "Not much. I work late."

Sawyer hopped down from the cabin, frowning. Over the sound of traffic, he shouted, "Schedule says you weren't working last night."

The driver just shook his head. "I took a shift from a bud."

"This buddy of yours have a name?"

"What's this about?"

Sawyer began to approach once more, his own hand resting against his holster. "Just asking questions. Nothing yet."

The man shifted uncomfortably. "You know what, how about I get my license. I'll show you I'm telling the truth."

This didn't make much sense, but the man began to move, jostling past Sawyer, nearly pushing the agent over the white line into traffic.

Sawyer cursed as the man slipped by. "We don't need your license right now," Sawyer said.

But the mechanic just waved a hand dismissively. "It's fine, it's fine. Here, just let me grab it."

Ilse tensed. Her heart pounded. He was picking up the pace. Sawyer suddenly lunged forward, trying to grab the man's wrist. But he shouted, and shoved the tall, sandy-haired agent.

Sawyer cursed, stumbling, and nearly fell in front of an oncoming sedan.

The vehicle swerved, leaning on its horn. Sawyer gather himself, stumbling back to safety on the shoulder.

But Reck was clambering into the cabin of his truck already. He slammed the door as Sawyer tried to reach it. Locked it before Sawyer could open it.

Ilse shouted, but he didn't listen. He gunned the engine.

Then, he floored the gas. Exhaust spewed into Ilse's face. A hot, stinking cloud of fumes and smoke. At the same time, their suspect leaned on his horn, clearing a path into the oncoming traffic.

Honking, spewing smoke, revving his engine, the scrapyard worker moved onto the highway.

Sawyer was already sprinting, racing back towards Ilse and shouting, "Get in the car! Back in the car!"

Ilse's heart leapt. She hurried into the passenger side as Sawyer also reached the vehicle.

Mr. Reck's large truck was swerving now. The half loaded junker shifted, sending sparks where the base scraped against the metal platform.

"That's not good," Ilse muttered. Sawyer followed her indicating finger and growled to himself.

"Careful, that thing is coming loose!”

Reck was picking up speed, faster, faster now, hastening away from the two agents. Ilse shouted as the truck veered sharply onto the highway, completing its turn along the offramp.

The fourth, rusted jalopy scraped and sparked, protesting where it dragged across the ground. Bits of rust and chunks of weathered metal went flying. They tapped against the windshield, like hailstones. Sawyer didn't even blink, but Ilse ducked with each sound, fearing the worst.

Sawyer picked up speed, trying to swerve around the large truck.

But their suspect noticed the move, and veered to the side, into the second lane, blocking Sawyer's progress.

"Careful!" Ilse shouted, "he's trying to run you off the road!"

Sawyer hit the brakes, veering sharply the other direction, trying to juke the bigger truck.

It worked, almost.

Sawyer's smaller car was too fast. He managed to slip alongside the bigger truck, but at the same time, Ilse heard a loud shattering sound. She looked back, her heart in her throat, watching as the rusted car finally fell, the chains suspending it snapping.

Other cars behind them were moving slowly, having spotted the erratic motion.

The rusted vehicle spun and tumbled, sending more pieces of metal flying. "Sawyer, careful!"

Tom spotted it a moment later. The truck was again trying to ram into them. Sawyer leaned on the horn, picking up the pace.

The truck bumped against Sawyer's door. A loud, scraping sound filled the car. They were nearly sent spinning. But Sawyer managed to keep control of the vehicle. He was knocked onto the shoulder of the road. The bigger truck kept trying to squeeze. It edged him against the concrete barrier, closer, closer. Only a foot between Ilse's door and the concrete. Only half a foot. A few inches.

Sawyer yelled, flooring the gas, and pulling in front of the truck just in time.

Ilse heard a loud shattering sound, and the truck hit their bumper, trying to spin them again. But once more, swerving to the left, Sawyer managed to maintain control.

Now they were in front of the truck.

"Ilse," Sawyer said, gritting his teeth, "You're not gonna like this. Hold on."

"Tom! Tom what are you—Tom!"

Ilse's shout was lost as Sawyer leaned on the horn and then slammed on the brakes in front of the truck. If he had thought this would stop the oncoming vehicle, he was sorely mistaken. Mr. Reck was not in the stopping mood.

But Sawyer seemed to realize this. The moment their bumpers hit, he floored the gas again. But just as quickly he stopped again.

Ilse jolted forward, then jerked back. She was certain she had whiplash.

Sawyer tried the move again, leaning on the horn and slamming on his brakes. Again, the bigger vehicle hit them from behind, and again, Sawyer absorbed some of the collision by flooring the pedal.

Slowly, painstakingly slowly, he was reducing the speed of both their vehicles.

In the distance, Ilse could hear sirens rapidly approaching. But they would be too late.

She glanced through the back windshield, which had shattered. She glimpsed the face of the mechanic. His cheeks were gaunt, his bloodshot eyes staring through the glass at them. He was shouting in his compartment, gesticulating wildly at Sawyer's car.

"He's not gonna stop, Tom!" she screamed.

Sawyer nodded once. He kept up the pace, faster, faster. And then he slammed the brakes again. And again, the truck behind them rammed into them, but this time, Reck floored his vehicle.

Suddenly, he was shoving their car, like a snowplow carving through flecks of ice.

Ilse's heart was in her throat. The sound of screeching, honking, whipping wind in her ears. She wanted to scream, but all she could do was brace herself, double checking, triple checking she was still buckled.

The truck behind them shoved them along the tarmac, faster, faster.

Suddenly, Sawyer tried to spin away, but it was too late. The oncoming truck was plowing them towards a curve in the road. Another concrete barrier. This time, it was going to slam them against it.

"Moron is gonna kill us both!" Sawyer bellowed. He was still trying to keep in line with the truck, to prevent it from getting away.

"Sawyer, let it go! Get us out of here!"

But Sawyer was too focused on the task. His eyes were the color of stubborn. And now it was showing. There were a couple of opportunities, Ilse felt certain, where Sawyer could've slipped to the left or right, allowing the truck to zoom past them. But then it would get away, going off the ramp again. Sooner or later police would catch it, but Sawyer wasn't in the mood to let him skate. She stared at her partner, wide-eyed in horror, at the way his hands tensed, the way his teeth were gritted. The way his jaw was clenched.

"Come on, baby," he was muttering. "Come on."

The truck kept speeding forward, threatening to sandwich them against a wall of concrete. Sawyer slammed the brakes as hard as he could. Their car jolted. But the motion behind them kept them going.

Still, the rubber of their tires, the weight of their own car, was serving as a buffer.

Were they slowing? It *felt* like they were slowing.

Sawyer's face was red, every muscle tensed. Ilse was shouting, and she couldn't even tell what she was saying. The truck was slowing. Painstakingly, with every inch, reducing in speed. But it was still carrying them towards the concrete—

Wham!

Ilse jolted forward hard. Her ribs protested. The air leapt from her lungs. She was punched in the face by a bag of white air bursting from the dashboard.

Her head slammed back against the headrest. Pain. Her whole face was filled with pain. The back of her head—pain. Her ribs. Pain.

She groaned, trying to move, dark spots and white lights dancing across her vision. For a moment, she thought for certain she was dead.

But dead people didn't experience this much bruising.

She tried to move. Her hands twitched. At least there was that. It meant she still had an intact spine.

She groaned, still blinking, and slowly her vision cleared. Steam wafted across the hood of their vehicle. Plumes of cottony white gusted over their car. Their windshield was gone. The back window was gone. The hood was crumpled, against the concrete.

But at least they hadn't been crushed. Sawyer, though, had been knocked unconscious by his air bag.

Ilse blinked a few times, groaning, and shaking her head. Slowly, she tested each of her fingers, her toes. Then tried to move.

Pain. But more of a dull, throbbing ache, as opposed to a lancing, sharp agony. Bruised, not broken. At least on first inspection.

She reached out, still dazed. The scent of the smoke from their hood, of oil, of metal reached her nose. Burning rubber soon joined in.

She jostled Sawyer's shoulder. "Tom!" she said. She tasted blood and realized she had bitten her lip. "Tom!" she said louder. She tested her lip. A shallow bite, thankfully. It didn't seem like she would need stitches.

She tried slapping him lightly on the face.

Sawyer groaned, blinking. His eyes snapped open. He stared at her for a moment, clearly discombobulated. "Rebekah?" he said, his eyes wide.

Ilse felt a jolt of embarrassment. That was his sister's name.

"No, Tom, it's Ilse."

Sawyer blinked a few times, shaking his head. He wasn't bleeding either. By slamming on the brakes, and thanks to the airbags, they'd been spared serious injury.

The truck behind them was still motionless, keeping them wedged up against the concrete. Sawyer's eyes blinked a couple more times, but then he suddenly seemed to realize where they were.

He let out a long groan. "Ilse? Shit. Is he—" Sawyer looked back. Then he cursed.

He ripped his buckle off. He shoved the airbag out of his way. He pushed open his door. This took a few tries as it was bent and wedged. With a groan of exertion, shouldering it, he opened the door and fell out onto the shoulder of the road.

As he got dazedly to his feet, glass fell off his arms, off his fingers. "Shit. Sorry, doc," Sawyer muttered. But even as he apologized, he ripped his gun from his holster. He stumbled towards the truck behind them.

Ilse peered in the rearview mirror. At least this was still intact.

The driver and the truck were motionless. His head bowed over the steering wheel. Gun in hand, Sawyer rotated around the cabin of the truck. "Get out with your hands up!" Sawyer was shouting.

The distant sound of sirens wasn't so distant anymore. Ilse thought she detected blue and red flashing in her mirror.

She groaned again but realized Sawyer might need her help. With a sigh of exhaustion, she shoved open the door, pushed out, and took stumbling steps towards the front of the truck, reaching for her own weapon, and with the other hand going for her handcuffs.

Mr. Reck moaned, sitting up. He had a nasty bruise forming over his eye and a superficial cut on his cheek. But otherwise, he seemed fine.

"Nearly killed us!" Sawyers shouted. "Get out. Now!"

Agent Tom Sawyer was not in a playing mood. Ilse stood behind her partner, allowing him to drag their suspect from the front seat, and put him on the ground.

Ilse handed her cuffs over as Sawyer, making sure nothing was broken on their suspect, twisted the man's arms behind his back.

"We have some questions." Sawyer's eyes flashed in fury, and he shot another look towards Ilse. "You okay?"

"You should've stopped," Ilse said. "I wish you'd listened to me."

Sawyer blinked, frowning. Then he let out a sigh, "Oh, you mean the car. Yeah, sorry. I knew we had him. We weren't going fast enough to get killed. Just a couple of bumps and bruises. I am sorry."

Ilse exhaled shakily. Sawyer had been doing this for long enough that she believed him. He probably calculated the whole thing. That didn't mean it wasn't terrifying. Didn't mean he wasn't being reckless. And now he was dragging her into it.

Then again, wasn't that what she had offered? To be with him in the pain? To help him?

She could still see that haunted look in his eyes when he'd first woken. Almost as if he thought he found himself in heaven and was finally gazing upon his sister after all those years.

She certainly hoped he didn't think of her as a sister. But she understood, dazed, confused, as he had woken, what connections his mind probably made.

More importantly, what he had clearly been thinking about for days now. Perhaps even years. Knowing a man like Tom, he hadn't stopped thinking about his sister's murder since it had happened.

She could still hear the grief in his tone, the way, as his vision had adjusted, his expression had clouded in disappointment. Not because it had been Ilse sitting there. But because his sister wasn't.

That was a man with deep grief.

And it had ended in two crumpled cars on the side of a highway.

Sawyer pulled their suspect to his feet.

The sirens had reached them now. Police cars were hastily pulling through the traffic, swerving or taking the shoulder and avoiding as much glass as they could.

The cavalry had arrived. But quite late.

Still, they had their guy.

CHAPTER SIXTEEN

There was a quiet *smack* as Ilse slapped the ice pack on her neck. She winced, tilting her head, and then staring in accusation across the table.

Amos Reck's bruises and superficial cut had already been tended to. Now he just sat there, glancing furtively about, and rubbing at the backs of his knuckles one at a time. His cuffs scraped against the metal table, eliciting a sound similar to the one accompanying the collision of his truck against their sedan. Both vehicles would eventually end up in one of the very scrapyards they were investigating, most likely.

Sawyer was sitting now. A rarity for him in an interrogation room. But he had twinged his back in the collision and was doing his best not to look in pain. This was interspersed by the occasional glare towards their suspect.

"I want to start by saying something..." Sawyer said.

Ilse shot him a look, but then winced, pressing the ice against her tweaked neck. The man across the table didn't look up.

"I said I want to say something."

The man sighed and then looked up.

Sawyer pointed at him. "You're a moron. An absolute idiot." Sawyer nodded, leaned back, winced, then crossed his arms in satisfaction as if he had accomplished what he had set out to do.

Ilse sighed. "Thank you for your contribution, Sawyer." She looked towards Reck. "You're connected to all three scrapyards where we found murder victims. You just tried to kill two federal agents. And you ran when you saw us. I might not state it in such callous terms, but I agree with my partner. You're in trouble, sir."

He shifted, his cuffs scraping against the metal table again. Ilse winced against the objectionable sound. A faint trickle of melted water was now dabbing at the top of her shirt. She could feel it threatening to slip down her back.

She lowered the ice pack onto the metal table. Condensation rapidly formed beneath it against the surface. Her fingers buzzed from the cold.

"So why did you kill them?" She figured a direct approach was probably the best. He'd certainly been direct when he'd rammed them.

Amos shook his head. "I didn't try to kill you! You pulled in front of me."

"You didn't stop!" Sawyer said with a growl.

Ilse sighed, massaging her nose. Sawyer had gone above and beyond. Well beyond, in order to stop Reck from fleeing. But now, he was more of a liability than anything. Getting their suspect riled up wouldn't help elicit a confession.

"What my partner means to say," Ilse began.

"You didn't stop," Sawyer interrupted. "That's what I mean to say."

The mechanic shook his head. "It's a free country. Your fault for parking in front of me while I was moving."

Sawyer said, "We told you we were feds. You bolted."

"No, I was just late for work."

Sawyer scoffed. Ilse crossed her arms.

Reck looked up, his red ringed eyes staring. "I didn't try to kill you. And I didn't kill anyone else," he added, in a higher pitched voice. "That's insane."

Ilse said, "You have access to each scrapyard. One of the owners, Mr. Connolly, told us you were delivering on the night Matthew Wagonmaker was killed."

"Who?" He shook his head and raised his cuffed hands. "I know Connolly. He's a drinking buddy. An asshole. But Matthew? Never heard of him. Does he work at the yard?"

"Are you feigning ignorance to deflect suspicion?" Ilse said, without missing a beat. Perhaps it was just the pain in her neck, but she had decided to keep him on the off foot this time. Gentle, comforting, assuaging was all well and good. But she drew a line when someone tried to run her off the road.

He said, "I'm not lying, lady. I didn't kill anybody. First thing I heard of it."

"Then why did you run?"

"I didn't."

Sawyer slammed a fist against the table, but then grit his teeth and massaged his elbow. He said, "Say their names. Say them. Janet Lee. Matthew Wagonmaker. Ian Hofster. That's your fault. You did this. And then like a coward you tried to run. You endangered a hundred more people on that highway. But of course, you don't care. You psychopath."

Reck looked genuinely offended. "How dare you!"

Sawyer tried to push from his seat. Ilse caught his arm and held him in place. "Maybe we should start from the top. Let's start with the most recent murder. Where were you last night? We already have an eyewitness placing you at the scrapyard."

"Last night? Someone took my shift. That's what I meant earlier."

"It's not what you said."

He blinked, his eyes still bloodshot beneath the bright light above. He shook his head, muttering darkly.

Ilse leaned in. Her fingertips nudged the cold ice pack. Her eyes fixed unblinking on his face. "Are you on something, Mr. Reck?"

He immediately shifted. He didn't look her in the eyes. He glanced in every direction but Ilse's. "What?"

"You heard me."

Sawyer snorted. "He's baked. High as a kite. Look at his eyes. Is that why you ran? Drugs?"

The man shifted uncomfortably, massaging his wrists. "I didn't run."

"Stop lying!" Sawyer snapped.

Reck looked miserable now. "Man, I need this job." he said it so quietly Ilse had to lean in to hear.

"So you try to kill FBI agents? You murder three people?" Sawyer pressed.

Reck shook his head violently and grit his teeth, suddenly trying to reach up and massage his upper spine. But his cuffs wouldn't let him. "I didn't kill anyone. It was an early morning. It's like I said, my buddy took my shift last night. I wasn't even at that scrapyard!"

"But you have access. We spoke to the owners. You can get in whenever you want."

"If *they're* with me," he countered. "Did you ask Connolly about that? He has to be looking over my shoulder. I'm not allowed in without one of them. Passcodes, locks. The truck is flagged. I can't just, like, sneak through something. I have to drive up the main road. They won't let me in without the manager there. That's how it works. My buddy did the job for me last night, anyway. I was taking care of my mother."

Sawyer snorted. "Yeah right."

"Dead serious. She has a condition. She needed me to pick up," he shot at glanced towards the door, "some medicine for her."

"Did you *consume* some of that medicine?" Sawyer said with a snort.

The man just shook his head. "Ask my mom. She knows where I was. Heck, she has one of those little door cams. You'll see me at her place. Ask my buddy, the one who took my shift. He'll vouch for me."

Ilse went still. This was no longer straight denial or speculation. These were verifiable claims. And as much as she disliked Reck, if he was telling the truth here, then there was no way he could've been in the scrapyard setting up the murder scene with a dismembered body.

"Your mother has a door cam?"

"Hell yeah she does."

"And it's going to show you, at what time?"

"Got there at five PM. It didn't leave until this morning for my shift."

Ilse felt like she'd been gut-punched. If this was true, there was no way he was their killer. The door cam would put him there, an hour away, right at the time of the murder. Even if he left the house again through the back and evaded the camera soon after, he wouldn't be able to get back in time. She frowned, pressing further. "Where's her house?"

He rattled off an address without hesitating. Then, seemingly sensing he had them cornered, he put out his chin defiantly, and in a belligerent tone declared, "Call her. Check it out!"

Sawyer pushed stiffly to his feet. He pointed a finger across the table. "You're an idiot."

Ilse sighed. The address he'd given was nearly an hour away from the scrapyard where Ian had been dismembered. It didn't work. If he was telling the truth, if he was on the door cam, and if his friend had taken his shift, there was no way. Unless they were in cahoots together. Maybe the two of them...

Ilse grimaced. But that wasn't what Rudiger had told them. Only Reck had a route that took him to all three spots. Besides, nothing in the MO of a narcissist, sadist serial killer, suggested that two men would ever want to commit the crimes as a team. It just didn't work for the profile. Still, they would have to check the whereabouts of this coworker...

But things were looking bleak.

Sawyer seemed to realize it too by the way he stomped back towards the door, shaking his head, and muttering beneath his breath.

Ilse said, "You might not have killed them—we'll check your alibi—but you almost killed us. I'm afraid you're going to be here for a while."

He stared at her, shocked, as if she had slapped him. Tears formed in his eyes, and he ducked his head, shoulders shaking as he cried at the table.

Ilse felt a jolt of sympathy. She couldn't help it. It was how she was wired. But compassion wouldn't make better choices for Mr. Reck. Compassion for *him* wouldn't help the many motorists he had endangered on the highway.

It hurt; it stung to see people like this. People who made such bad choices. People she wanted to help, but no matter what she did, it wouldn't undo the decisions they made.

Prisons had psychologists too. Hell, prisons had people. It didn't take much for a little bit of kindness, a little bit of love to go a long way. It worked with her clients. But sometimes, it didn't.

It wouldn't work with Sawyer, apparently. And she wasn't sure if someone like Mr. Reck would ever respond to kindness.

But still, she could try.

She took the ice pack, moved across the table, and slipped it beneath his hands.

She patted him on the shoulder, and without a word turned, leaving the interrogation room, and the crying mechanic behind her.

CHAPTER SEVENTEEN

The survivor pressed his fingers against the moldered wood, testing the sturdiness.

It flecked away beneath his fingers. His face twisted in a sneer, and he peeled more shavings, allowing them to tumble to the cement stoop at his feet. The scent of mold also lingered on the air, the blackened wood whispering of neglect and water damage. He turned, peering up the side street towards the bakery across the street. An older woman pushed a wheeled cart, moving ever so slowly.

He waited, leaning back casually, allowing her to pass out of line of sight before returning to his work.

With his left hand, he reached into his waistband and pulled out the pry-bar he'd brought from home.

"Discarded with some old paint cans, wasn't it?" he whispered to himself, then nodded, smiling. "Yes, yes—the things these folk throw away." He slipped the pry-bar between the doorjamb once he was certain the coast was clear.

The shadows of the looming buildings on either side of him kept him cradled in darkness. He grunted, pushing on the bar.

The wood began to give. He paused, exhaling faintly, feeling sweat prickling along his cheeks and forehead. Then, he returned to his efforts.

He used his left hand as a pivot point and leaned the rest of his body into the motion. The wooden door didn't so much creak as grumble. The wood was old, worn, weathered, and rotten. Clumps fell where he pried.

Eventually, he'd worn through enough of the wood to display the locking mechanism.

Locks he knew.

He had an affinity for the devices.

He leaned in, studying the lock, inhaling the rotten scent of the door. His finger found the casing and he gripped it entirely.

As his fingers touched against the cold metal, a flare of pain shot down his right arm. He hissed, wincing and leaning against the door again, his head pressing to the rough surface. Phantom pain some called it.

A pain in the ass was *his preferred* term. Or, at least, a pain in the arm.

But the pain wasn't just physical. It also brought a sort of mental anguish too. He exhaled shakily as his fingers gripped the lock, memories coming past the barriers in his mind, flooding his subconscious. “Make him pay,” he whispered to himself. He nodded, his face scraping against the wood, his eyeball widening from the way his skin stretched, his cheek flattened. “Make them pay,” he said, louder.

He'd already chosen the next debtor. They all owed him a debt. An arm and a leg, some might say.

He was sick of these people skating about without answering for what they did. The first little monster had killed someone in a hydraulic press. Next, the doe-eyed boy. He'd felt a jolt of pity seeing how young he'd been. But the boy hadn't shown any pity towards the woman he'd killed, had he?

And the last one—the worst of all. Multiple people injured, dismembered in a carnival ride gone horrible.

He seethed, spittle flecking his lips and the door. He sobbed against the wood, briefly, allowing the pain to subside as it eventually, always did. It never left completely, but rather lingered, clinging to him like his own personal mold. A little reminder, a demon in his ear.

“It'll be a good one,” he spoke against the door. He pushed away from the frame now, his hand still gripping the exposed locking mechanism. “He'll be by soon enough. I promise.” He nodded to himself, as if accepting the oath.

Then, with a grunt and a groan, he ripped the locking mechanism from the already disassembled doorframe. He pushed at the wood and, slowly, on old hinges, the door swung in.

He shot another look up the alley.

No witnesses; no one was paying attention. They never did, anyhow.

As he stepped into the dark room, he inhaled with a faint shiver. No scent on the air... but that was what had killed the last tenant, wasn't it? A carbon monoxide leak... And the bastard landlord hadn't done shit about it.

No... The survivor had gone to great lengths to find the landlord's schedule. Had set up a fake phone, a fake name and even a fake credit report to ask for a tour of this run-down, moldered, rot and rat-infested hellhole called a starter-home.

Now... all he had to do was wait for the man to show up.

The survivor looked around the small, space, studying the old furniture, the bare, concrete floor. A few chairs, one cushioned seat.

He preferred the cement. He lowered to the ground, back against a brick wall, and leaned his head against the edge of a cold fireplace. Tick-tock... Just a little time. A little bit of patience. The cheese was placed.

The spring loaded.

The rat would come.

CHAPTER EIGHTEEN

Ilse stood outside the interrogation room, frowning towards where Agent Sawyer was smacking a vending machine. The agent's hand already stained the glass, but he continued his insistent pats, trying to dislodge a bag of chips that had been caught.

Ilse sighed, moving up the hall towards where the sandy-haired man stood hunched in the shadows.

Another *whack* of his palm against the glass, and she flinched. Her fingers flicked towards her ear, brushing her hair.

She thought, briefly, horribly, of her father. His parole hearing was looming. She needed to get tickets, book a hotel. Needed to prepare for the meeting. Perhaps even write a speech. But the longer this case went on, the harder it would be for her to be there for the parole. Her frustrations were mounting in this case.

Tom was clearly feeling similar.

"Come on!" Tom snapped, administering another *thwack.*

"That's not the suspect," Ilse said quietly, standing off, away.

Tom shot her a look, frowned, and returned his attention to the vending machine. His eyes kept darting in the glass, though, tracking her in the reflection. He seemed distant, unable to focus. Back there, in the interrogation room, he'd been at his worst behavior. Agent Sawyer was a professional—at least, as long as she'd known him.

But things were growing unhinged. He wasn't acting like himself. She could see him behaving more and more recklessly.

Ilse sighed, crossing her arms and leaning against the wall. "I think we need to talk."

"About *the case*," Tom replied just as quickly. "Obviously." He turned, giving up on his chips and glaring towards the interrogation room door beyond them. "I have Dawes checking out his alibi. He's trying to get that doorcam footage from the mother."

Ilse nodded. "Good. I think it'll check out."

Sawyer rubbed at his chin. "We don't *know* that. He tried to kill us."

"He ran us off the road. If he really had wanted to kill us, he would've backed over us when were standing on the shoulder."

Sawyer grumbled. "Maybe he was just too dumb to think of that."

Ilse grimaced but shook her head. "I don't know about that, Tom. I think—I think maybe he's not our guy. We won't know until the alibi checks out. But did you notice the way he kept stroking his knuckles?"

"I guess."

"He's right-handed," Ilse said simply. "I was paying close attention. He's right-dominant. The coroner suggested the killer was probably left-handed."

Sawyer sighed. "Could be faking."

Ilse shook her head. "Possibly. We'll know if his alibi doesn't check out... But if it does?"

Sawyer gave a harrumph, but then nodded. "I know, I know," he muttered. "Due diligence."

"Exactly. No sense in sitting idly by while we wait for that footage."

Sawyer shrugged, his flannel rubbing against the glass vending machine door. "So what are you thinking, doc? What's the ace up your sleeve?"

Ilse sighed, trying not to think about her father still. She couldn't blame Sawyer for being distracted if she was going to let externalities also influence her ability to focus. She winced as she shifted, massaging her neck and slowly rolling her bruised shoulder. It hurt when she cocked an elbow, so she tried to keep her arms straight at her side.

"I-I don't know exactly," she said slowly, "but it's clear each accident our three victims were involved in either injured or killed someone due to carelessness or negligence."

Sawyer grunted.

"So maybe... instead of looking at means, we look at motive..."

"So no more scrapyard employees?"

"Exactly. Maybe we should look at the survivors of the accidents, or their family members. Anyone who might have a strong enough dislike or disdain of our victims to go to such lengths. Maybe with a welding or metal-working background."

Sawyer looked in a bad mood again. "Sounds like a lot of typing," he muttered.

She winced. Nodded.

"Sounds like we might need help..."

She tried to look sufficiently chastised. "He's *really* good at what he does, Tom."

Sawyer sighed.

"He could get the information we want in half the time we could. A tenth of the time."

Another, longer, resigned sigh.

Sawyer muttered something that sounded suspiciously like, *but I don' wanna.* But then he reached into his pocket and with slow, laborious movements, he pulled out his phone.

***

Ilse listened as Rudiger's cheerful voice buzzed over the phone's speaker as he talked them through the file. "Stop clicking, Tommy!" he exclaimed, "I haven't locked the columns yet."

Tom hesitated, finger hovering over his keyboard. Ilse and Tom had found the breakroom and were now lingering behind a locked door with a chair placed conveniently beneath the handle. The lock and chair had been Sawyer's doing—he simply didn't want to be bothered by any other law enforcement officers.

Ilse tried to smile and nod through the large glass windows as officers moved past. She didn't want anyone to think they had a hostage situation on their hands.

It was a close call, too, given Sawyer's ever-reddening face and heightening frustration.

"Tommy, I said *stop*!" Rudiger piped over the speaker

"I didn't do anything that time!"

"Yes—yes you did. You're not *clicking* but you're moving the shared cursor. Just hands off, big guy."

Sawyer reached out, unplugging his mouse from his computer. "There!" Tom said. "The cursor is all yours."

Ilse waited hesitantly, staring at the screen. Rudiger let out a little sigh. Then, the techie said, "Tommy... Did you unplug that external hard drive?"

Sawyer hesitated, glanced back down, then cursed. He quickly readjusted the cables and said, "No—must be something on your end, Ruds."

The voice snorted over the phone. "Likely," it said. "Alright, now pay attention, my dears, while Uncle Rudy weaves a tapestry of a tale."

Sawyer blinked. "What?"

"Just watch," Rudiger huffed.

Sawyer reached for the phone sitting on the desk and lowered the volume by about half. Ilse choked back a chuckle. It wasn't difficult, though, as her gaze landed on the computer screen. Through the windows facing the street, she noticed traffic was falling off. The afternoon was now quickly approaching evening.

And with the darkening skies, her countenance endeavored to match the bleak outlook as she studied the names on the screen.

Rudiger had combed through mentions on police reports, plaintiffs and defendants in the subsequent lawsuits, following the accidents. He'd gone through employee records and worker compensation. And then, he'd compiled all the names on one giant list, complete with their phone numbers, addresses, dates of birth, and drivers' licenses.

All of it had taken the computer whiz a few hours.

“So,” Rudiger said, “when I click this bar, it reduces the list based on criminal record or history of violence. See that? Tommy? See?”

“I see it Rudiger.”

“Now you try.”

Sawyer reached for his mouse. “Umm... It's not working.”

Ilse tapped his shoulder and whispered, “Plug the mouse back in.”

Sawyer winced, flashed a thumbs up, then hastily began to follow the prior instructions. “The spreadsheet is kinda slow,” Sawyer said hurriedly to cover the brief lull. “Think there might be a bad connection or something.”

“Tommy, I'm watching you on the webcam. You unplugged the mouse. Now—see what I did? Click that.”

Sawyer frowned, raising a finger to rub at the small little camera lens on top of his laptop screen but then he returned his attention back to the spreadsheet.

“What we have here,” Rudiger said in summary, “Is a web of would-be suspects. When we narrow the list based on criminal record or violent tendencies, we have a list of five. But one is deceased and two are currently in prison.”

As he spoke, names disappeared on the spreadsheet before Ilse's eyes.

She stared at the screen. “Two names? That's all?”

Rudiger chuckled. “That's all my dear, but wait, there's more. This one—see here, Sally Philips? She was injured in the Mr. Wagonmaker's car crash. She no longer walks. Which is sad, but in this moment good for her.”

“Yeah, no way she's behind this,” Ilse murmured. “What about Juan Lopez?”

“Ah, yes,” said Rudiger. “Mr. Lopez is our Cinderella, I believe.

Just remember to give him a smack on the lips before midnight."

Ilse paid attention as Sawyer clicked on Lopez's name, bringing them to a driver's license photo of a man with hooded eyes and a lazy smile. He had short-cut, prickly hair and the scruff of a man who didn't care to tend to his facial hair. His eyes were bright, though, and intelligent.

"What's Mr. Lopez's relation to the victims?"

Rudiger's tone become a lot less coy. "He was the husband of the woman who Matthew Wagonmaker accidentally killed in that car crash. Court records show a disturbance where he tried to charge the witness box."

"Shit," Sawyer said. "He tried to attack Mr. Wagonmaker?"

Rudiger continued in that ominous tone. "He *did* attack. And by the looks of things, this week he finished what he'd started two years ago."

"What was his arrest record for?" Ilse asked. "A courtroom incident?"

"No—no, the judge was lenient in that case. But about a year later, Mr. Lopez was caught boosting cars. He spent six months in prison. In fact, he only got out two weeks ago."

Ilse stared at the screen.

Just then, Sawyer's phone buzzed. He glanced down, studying something for a moment, but then he lifted the device and displayed it so Ilse could see.

It was a multimedia message sent by Agent Dawes. On it, Ilse watched as a video feed displayed, clearly, Mr. Reck stumbling up a sidewalk after parking half on the curb. He was drunk. The door was answered and then Mr. Reck disappeared from view.

The video kept playing, but sped-up, reaching 10x. The car remained parked on the curb. No one came or left the house through the front door. Ilse stared at the timestamp as the video kept playing.

"That's the door footage?" Ilse asked.

Sawyer bobbed his head. "Mr. Reck was at his mother's place during the time of the attack. Just like he said."

"Unless he used a different car..." Ilse replied cautiously. But even as she said it, she didn't buy it. Perhaps he *was* pretending to be drunk in the video. Perhaps his mother and his coworker were both lying for him. Perhaps he was faking to be right-handed and had pretended to be left-handed in a murder just to trick them. Perhaps, in all of it, he was playing them...

But it was just too many coincidences. Too much to place on the shoulders of a man like Mr. Reck. A man that tried to ram two feds. A man who couldn't even keep a car on his flatbed. Mr. Reck didn't strike Ilse as a criminal mastermind. The possibility was there, but a far more likely possibility was now staring them in the face.

She looked away from Sawyer's upheld phone, studying the laptop screen once more.

Juan Lopez stared out at her, his lazy smile, his hooded eyes, his easy demeanor—even in a photo—all culminating in a sense of severe distrust.

The man's gaze was alert, attentive, but hidden by a disarming expression.

"And get this," Rudiger said suddenly, the excitement returning to his voice. "I double-checked but it looks like in his Sunday baseball league, our Cinderella is *left-handed*."

Sawyer snorted, already pushing to his feet. "Well then," he muttered. "Guess it's time to speak to Mr. Lopez."

"Have fun!" Rudiger called over the phone.

"Thanks, Rudy!" Ilse said.

Sawyer hung up, slipping the phone into his pocket, closing his laptop lid, and hastening towards the door to move the chair.

CHAPTER NINETEEN

"Tom," Ilse said quickly, glancing towards the flashing red button on the radio receiver in the middle of the dashboard. Agent Sawyer was still driving, hastening down the highway in the direction of Mr. Lopez's address. "Tom!" Ilse repeated, louder.

Her partner jolted, glancing at her. "What was that?"

She pointed towards the radio again. Tom frowned, reaching out and clicked the receiver.

A muffled voice spoke on the other end. "We have a hit on that APB of yours, Sawyer."

Ilse perked up.

"On Juan Lopez's vehicle?"

"That's the one," the voice replied.

"Where is it heading?" Sawyer said.

Ilse waited, rigid.

The voice replied, "It's at Mountains Scrapyard. Owned by a Benjamin Connolly. I can move in to apprehend."

"No," Sawyer said hurriedly. "We're only a few minutes away. Stay there." Tom clicked off the radio and merged to cross traffic to a chorus of blaring horns.

"He went back to the second crime scene?" Ilse said, frowning as she spoke.

"Looks like it," Sawyer replied. "You said he was a narcissist. Don't they like returning to the scenes of their crimes?"

"Usually when there's family or grieving friends nearby."

"Or law enforcement," Sawyer said.

Ilse nodded as Sawyer floored the gas, taking a ramp, and turning away from the city to head to the outskirts once more.

Ilse's fingers drummed against the window. It all fit. A left-handed killer with a motive. Mr. Lopez had lost his wife in a car crash that had seen their second victim go completely free.

She sighed in frustration, shaking her head.

Sawyer continued to pick up speed, heading further away from the dusty horizon of gray and glass.

Out here, where the buildings were sparser, even as they

maneuvered in the direction of a local junkyard, Ilse found that she could think more clearly. The less stress, the less people, the more thoughts her mind seemed to allow her a modicum of rest.

Then again, *too* few people and things could get weird. Ilse shifted in her chair, wondering if that had been her father's problem.

Too few people. He'd lived in a house on a lake on a couple of acres. The parole was coming quickly. Sooner or later, she would have to make plans. Would have to book a hotel.

Part of her wanted to avoid it entirely. But another part of her felt ready to face the old man.

This time, she refused to let him get the upper hand.

"There it is," Sawyer said suddenly, interrupting her train of thoughts. Ilse looked through the windshield, following his pointed finger over the steering wheel. They were rapidly approaching Connolly's scrapyard. An unmarked sedan was on the side of the road. Sawyer waved as they passed.

"The cops coming too?" Ilse said.

Sawyer muttered, "Don't want them spooking anyone. Besides, they're not going to be far."

Ilse begged to differ. As she peered into the rearview mirror, watching the car dwindle into the background, she couldn't help but feel that if gunshots resounded, the police reinforcements would take far too long to reach the agents to be of any use.

But, regardless, Sawyer seemed to have made his choice.

Again, as they entered through the old, rusted gates, nudging the unlocked fence open with the hood of their car, the bumper contacting a support pole, Ilse was reminded of the broken chains, the missing barbed wire, the absent cameras. This junkyard was hardly a reputable place.

Perhaps that was why Mr. Lopez had returned to the crime scene.

Ahead, as they trundled to a halt on the side of the road near a stack of old, gutted automobiles, Ilse heard a commotion.

Sawyer hesitated, frowning, then muttered, "Sounds like a fistfight. We better get going."

Ilse followed Sawyer out of the car. The two of them hastened towards the noise. Sawyer took the lead, just a few paces ahead of her. He allowed his hand to drift towards his weapon as he took long strides across the dusty path. They moved past the familiar office that Ilse had despised on her first time through. Up ahead, Ilse spotted two employees in blue overalls interrupting a man with close-cut, shaved hair.

What Ilse had initially taken for the sound of fighting was actually the sound of two junkyard workers trying to drag Mr. Lopez from his perch on top of one of the metal gates. He was just out of reach though and laughed as the two men below him grunted in exertion, jumping to try to snag a foot, or poking at him with a long broomstick.

He wasn't going anywhere. Not just because he was out of reach, but because, by the looks of things, he had chained himself to the fence. Both of his ankles were secured with handcuffs, the metal cuffs looped through the gate.

"You've been up there long enough!" shouted Samuel Jerome who Ilse recognized from their last visit. The old, white whiskered scrapyard worker tried to smack the man with his broom handle.

Mr. Lopez just lifted his leg a bit. The broom missed, ricocheting off the fence. Lopez couldn't lift his leg too much, on account of the restraining cuffs but he had enough range of movement to dodge the broom swipes.

Lopez said, "I'm just enjoying the view. It's been a long time coming!"

As Ilse and Sawyer hastened forward, she recognized their suspect from his driver's license picture. The same sort of hooded gaze. The same sort of lazy smile. He had bright, clever eyes. The eyes of a man who was often used to being in control.

Ilse didn't recognize one of the junkyard employees, but the older one, Mr. Samuel, poked up with his broom again. "I gave you a few hours, to be kind. But you can't be here when Mr. Connolly gets back! I'm going to have to get the bolt cutters and remove those cuffs if you don't do it yourself!"

Mr. Lopez laughed. "You saw me swallow the key. You better go get cutting."

The junkyard employees grumbled to each other, rattling the fence but failed to dislodge the man perched at the pinnacle.

Lopez glanced over the junkyard employees, his eyes fixating on where Ilse and Sawyer approached. "Looks like we have guests," he called out.

The others turned to examine the new arrivals.

Ilse waved a hand in greeting. Sawyer's hand was still on his holster, his eyes refusing to leave where Mr. Lopez sat.

Ilse kept her cool. None of it really made sense. She decided to reserve judgment until she could parse out what motives were at play in this unusual space.

She tried to do just that by saying, "Hello gentlemen. We seem to have a situation. What's going on?"

Samuel turned to scowl at her. "This hooligan has chained himself to our fence for like five hours. Won't leave."

Ilse nodded and gave a commiserating smile in what she hoped would placate. She turned slowly to face their suspect sitting on the fence. He was smiling, his eyes twinkling with amusement. But she had to remember what she'd read in the file. He had tried to assault Matthew in a courtroom. His wife had been killed in the car crash. He had a criminal record for boosting cars. And with those handcuffs, it was clear that he preferred his left hand. He kept adjusting the chains with it.

"Juan Lopez?" she said, nodding in greeting.

He blinked in surprise, but then his lips twisted into a Cheshire grin. "You know who I am? You don't look like cops. I thought you guys were gonna call the police."

Samuel shook his head. "We didn't. I was about to. I don't care what your sob story is. You need to leave. You said you would."

Mr. Lopez shook his head. "I said I would eventually leave. I just didn't say when."

Samuel scowled. "I did. I didn't mind you sitting there when the boss wasn't here. But Connolly's coming within the hour." Samuel scratched his chin, then glanced at Ilse. "You're not cops. Why are the feds here again?"

Ilse nodded. "Good question. Mr. Lopez, do you know why we're here?"

She studied him carefully, trying to pick up any twitch, any hint, any movement. For the moment, from where she stood, she didn't spot a gun. At least there was that. Plus, for some reason, he had positioned himself like a duck on open waters. If he tried anything, Sawyer would take him out far quicker than he could attack them.

"If I knew, I wouldn't look so dumbfounded. Why are you here?"

Sawyer raised a hand, gesturing firmly. "Get down."

Lopez shook his head. "I can't. I wasn't lying. I swallowed the key." Lopez shrugged, frowning in thought. "I think I saw that in a movie one time. Let me tell you, it does not go down easy. Next time I might bring a juice box."

Ilse studied the man. Brash, clearly amused with himself. Narcissist? Bold. He knew how to enter the junkyard. And he sat on a fence facing the same direction where the car with the second victim had been discovered. Was this the behavior of their killer? He'd certainly been escalating—getting more and more over the top with his kills.

"We are here for *you*," Ilse said, deciding to play it slow "and you are here because you wanted to see your handiwork."

He's shrugged. "Not sure what you mean."

Sawyer was circling around the fence now. The lanky agent kept glancing from side to side, as if trying to spot the trap. But there didn't seem to be any. Lopez seemed content to just sit on his fence, staring towards the rows of automobiles. Every time he glanced over, he smirked again.

Samuel rattled the fence. He tried to swipe with his broom again. No avail.

"Something amusing?" Ilse called out.

Mr. Lopez pointed. "That's where he died, right? Did it hurt? I hope so. I told that judge," Lopez said, still forcing his grin, but his tone tightening, "that he should throw the book at that little maniac. Mr. Big Black Robes wouldn't hear it. He threatened to lock me up. And I said I would lock myself up if he would just take care of the boy."

Lopez shrugged. "So here I am. Locked up and enjoying the view. Besides, I can't tell you how much I liked reading the news over the last couple of days."

Sawyer was starting to climb the fence. Mr. Lopez hadn't noticed yet. Ilse kept his attention. "The news? I can't say I've been paying much attention."

Lopez waved towards the spot with the cars. "You have a firsthand view," he said. "Not all of us are so lucky."

"You're here to see where Matthew was killed?"

Lopez smirked. "Exactly. No crime against looking."

"We're not here because we're worried you were looking," Ilse replied.

The man on the fence crossed his arms, shrugging down at her. "So why are you here?"

"We'd like to speak with you," Ilse said.

Lopez snorted. "I know what that's code for. What you think I did it? Killed the kid?"

She blinked at the forthright question. No hesitation, no quaver to his voice. He just said it.

He snorted now, turning his head back and laughing. A clear, resonant sound. "Holy crap, you think I killed him? I thought this was a serial case. I noticed something else about a couple of other victims."

Ilse said, "You know about the case?"

By now, the scrapyard workers were glancing between the two of them, like spectators at a tennis match. Sawyer was still crawling up the fence from the other side, out of Mr. Lopez's line of sight.

Ilse was having a hard time getting a read on the guy. Far too confident. Far too amused. Far too easy going. Was he the serial killer? Narcissists and psychopaths often didn't have the same resonance for fear that most people did.

She glanced at the cuffs again, though. He had locked them in tight. What was he playing at? Why was he sitting on a fence in the middle of the junkyard? Was he telling the truth? Was he really here just to admire the murder spot?

"It doesn't look good; you're sightseeing a crime scene," she said, trying a different track.

He shook his head. "So sue me. Granted, I have it on good authority that doesn't work."

Ilse's expression flickered into a frown. "Mr. Lopez," she said, "did you know Janet Lee?"

He paused, considering it, then said, "I think she was the first victim. I wasn't paying much attention before little Matthew got it. But yeah. I think I've heard of her."

Ilse nodded. "You have an alibi for Monday?"

He looked at her. "Not a single one," he said.

She nodded. "What about the last few days?"

He paused, considering this. "I live at home, alone, thanks to the little devil that died over there. I don't really have friends. I don't much go out. I guess you could say I have absolutely no alibi whatsoever." He chuckled. "Probably not the best thing to say to a fed. So you think I killed him? You really think I killed the killer?"

Again, Ilse was struck at how cavalier he was acting. Nothing about his tone or posture suggested he was worried. Maybe he just didn't care. Or maybe she was missing something. Sawyer had now reached the man's feet. There was a quiet click as Sawyer used his own handcuff key. A second later, he pulled the chain off Lopez's leg.

Now, Juan noticed what was going on. "Hey, get off me!"

Sawyer didn't even bother to reply. He was already moving for the next cuff. Mr. Lopez didn't make it easy, shifting his foot around in every direction. So instead of going for the cuff around the ankle,

Sawyer just went for the one chained to the fence. He unhooked it, unlocked it, and allowed it to fall free of the metal mesh.

"Go away," Lopez said. "Get off me!"

Sawyer, still clinging to the fence with one hand, shot a look of grim satisfaction in Ilse's direction. Then, casually, he reached up and shoved Mr. Lopez in the middle of the back.

The man yelped and tumbled off the fence.

He hit the dirt with a *thump*. He stumbled a few steps, half crouched, absorbing the impact. He landed on one knee, a hand scraping through the dust.

Sawyer hopped off the fence and circled it through the exit to approach Lopez from behind.

Ilse approached from the front. The two of them stood on either side of the dusty man. He patted at his clothes, clearing the air with a hand. He glanced between of the two of them, still no sign of the nervousness Ilse was expecting.

He held up his hands. "Whatever, lady. I wanted to see where he died. This wasn't about you guys. I didn't kill him."

"Where were you this week?" Ilse said.

"I just told you. I don't have a life. It was taken from me. I'm just having some fun. Call it a little bit of sweet revenge."

"Revenge," Ilse said. "That *is* what I'm calling it."

Mr. Lopez just snorted. "Whatever. I didn't kill them."

Mr. Jerome leaned in, muttering beneath his breath so Ilse could hear, "He was up there for like six hours. Every now and then he started laughing. When he thought we weren't looking he started crying."

Lopez bristled. "I did *not* cry."

Samuel just shrugged and gave a significant tilt of his bushy eyebrows.

Ilse huffed, studying the fence and then looking back towards the cavalier survivor of the car crash from two years ago. "You say you didn't kill Matthew. But you also say you have no alibi."

He shrugged. "Innocent until proven guilty. At least that's what my favorite TV shows tell me. You have a different policy?"

Ilse just pressed doggedly on. "You were cited threatening Mr. Wagonmaker. You tried to attack him in the courthouse."

Sawyer was edging in from behind Mr. Lopez. Sawyer had his own cuffs out now. He was waiting, though, it seemed, for Ilse to conclude her line of questioning. And for the moment, Lopez just remained still, motionless, hands at his sides, making no effort to flee.

"Words were said," Lopez replied. "But they were just words. It was that little demon that killed someone." He jabbed his finger through the air towards where the automobile had been parked a couple of nights ago. He glared at Ilse now, some of his veneer cracking to show hurt in his eyes.

Ilse studied him. He didn't seem to pose a threat. Even Tom was lingering back, allowing him to speak before cuffing him.

He had chained himself to a fence. Hardly the act of a particularly inconspicuous, secretive killer. But he had means, motive, and opportunity. He was the prime suspect. And he was left-handed.

That had to cinch the deal, didn't it?

As she considered it, Ilse could feel her options rapidly dwindling. She didn't want to rush the case. But she also knew the longer they tarried, the more difficult it would be to book a trip to Germany. The harder it would be to focus on her father's parole hearing.

This wasn't a good reason to rush things. But it was a true one.

Samuel was moving away from the feds now, heading back towards that small office. Sawyer was shooting Ilse looks, as if waiting for permission to arrest the guy.

Ilse said, "It's hard to believe you," she tugged at her sleeves, "when you seem so cavalier about his death."

Lopez didn't bat an eyelid. "I could lie to you, to make my case for me. But I don't want to. I'm glad he's dead. He deserved to die. He was young. But young people aren't the same as they used to be. Everyone's entitled. Selfish. The officers didn't breathalyze him. He was drunk and he killed my wife. All I can hope is he suffered a little bit before going. And so yeah, I came here to see where he died. To celebrate. It's been a while since I've had something that I enjoyed."

His eyes flickered as he said this last part. There was a mean but also sad tint to his gaze.

Ilse said, "Mind if I see your hands?

He stared at her.

"We could just handcuff you," she said.

With a sigh, he raised his hands for her to examine.

She studied the fingertips. No calluses. The fingers themselves were small, thin, not the fingers of a metalworker not the fingers of someone used to hard labor.

That didn't mean that he wasn't the killer. But it was a hint they had either missed the profile or were missing something right now.

It should have been a slam-dunk. She knew that. The evidence all lined up. So what was she going off of?

Gut instinct?

He had all but admitted that he'd killed Matthew. By his own words he was glad the boy was dead. He had no remorse. No regret. He enjoyed talking about it. Hell, he had admitted to coming to the murder scene just to see where his wife's killer had died.

He was the one who did it. It was him. Wasn't it?

Ilse shot Sawyer look. "What do you think?"

Sawyer seemed relieved to finally be brought back into the fold. He said, "This is what I think."

He grabbed Mr. Lopez's wrists, pulling them behind his back. Sawyer's cuffs appeared. A couple of seconds, a couple of *clicks* later, and Mr. Lopez was standing handcuffed with his arms behind his back, still flashing that lazy smile of his, as if he didn't care whether he lived or died. Didn't care if they arrested him or let him go free. He just didn't seem to care at all. Except when he glanced in the direction of Matthew's crime scene.

Then his eyes would mist, but he would force a smile. He was trying to find a way to be happy. But it wasn't there. Not in his eyes. Not in the way he twisted and turned. Not in the way he went rigid every time Sawyer tried to prod him forward.

This man was projecting confidence, charm. He was callous and cavalier.

But really, what scared Ilse most, was how familiar the look in his eyes was.

A look of pain.

The same look Sawyer had.

A look of agony that had festered far too long without help. Without opening up. Without vulnerability.

And this time, by the looks of things, it had led to a murder spree.

Sawyer was jostling Mr. Lopez forward, pushing him down the dirt road away from the fence. As Sawyer and Lopez passed, Ilse's hand shot out. She caught Sawyer by the wrist and stared at him.

He looked back at her, his eyebrows rising in query.

"Be smart," Ilse said faintly. "You'll be smart, won't you?"

Sawyer wrinkled his nose in confusion. He said, "I'll try to be. You okay, doc?"

Ilse glanced towards the cuffed man Sawyer was pushing. She wanted to be okay. But she was scared. She couldn't really say why.

CHAPTER TWENTY

Sunny O'Leary stared at the door to his smallest rental property. It was broken. Someone had taken the lock.

He scowled, stomping forward up the alley, grumbling to himself. Damn metal thieves. He couldn't imagine a door handle and locking mechanism would fetch much more than a few bucks. He certainly hadn't paid more than that.

He grimaced, shaking his head, and spitting off to the side. The spittle darkened a gray wall behind some dumpsters.

He turned to face the door of his smallest rental unit. Not that impressive. Certainly not beautiful. But it made him a pretty penny. Which was kind of the point.

He pushed through the door, frowning at where splintered wood scattered across the doorstep. What else had they taken? He didn't usually leave much behind. The rentals came furnished but the furniture was all secondhand anyway.

"Mr. Johnson?" he called out into the house. "Hello?" He projected a cheerful voice. Certainly not how he was feeling but in the real estate game, one had to know how to turn it on when required.

He glanced around the entry room.

He couldn't see anyone. He'd arranged to meet with a prospective tenant a few days ago. The tenant was supposed to be there ten minutes before. What if he was the asshole that had stolen the lock?

Sunny's eyes narrowed in suspicion. "Mr. Johnson!" he called, louder now.

No response.

He grumbled to himself, looking around the space.

There was some mold damage by the door, over the fireplace. The fireplace was a complete gimmick as there was no chimney. Once, a tenant had actually tried to burn something in the hearth but had smoked out the whole house.

Another time, there had been a carbon monoxide issue. The alarms had been fine. It wasn't his fault the tenant hadn't read the small print—batteries not included.

Batteries were expensive. It was the tenant's shitty fault he had suffocated. Sunny shook his head, scanning the place, his eyes traveling over the furniture.

This was one of the reasons it was so hard to rent this place. It kept showing up when people searched the address.

He'd been hopeful this would be a positive business relationship with a new tenant. On the phone the guy had seemed so eager. But where was he?

Probably off somewhere with a doorknob.

He sighed, but then paused, trying not to breathe too deeply. The scent of mold was really quite strong. A little bit of paint, though, would cover the water damage. A little more paint, and the smell of rot would disappear for a bit. At least long enough to sign a lease. He wasn't made of money. It wasn't his job to build a custom, luxury house for cheap-ass renters.

He just provided the space.

Of course, he wouldn't be caught dead replacing an entire piping system. Perish the thought.

He paused as he looked around the space. Then heard a faint noise coming from the other room. A quiet, scratching sound. Shivers went up his spine.

He hated rats. Had even checked into an extermination service. Way too much money. Nearly half a month of rent. He was already behind. He needed a tenant, badly. Maybe a poison tablet set out over a couple of days would take care of the problem.

He listened to the scratching, followed by a sniffling, shuffling sound.

A shadow darted across the floor. About the size of a bread loaf. The shadow disappeared into a crack beneath the window.

Sunny winced. That had been a big one. Maybe double the poison. A couple of traps. But those cost money. He would have to write it into the tenant's new contract.

He sighed, shaking his head and turning slowly.

And then he went still.

There was a man sitting against the wall behind the couch.

Sunny hadn't seen him when he'd first entered. The man just sat on the floor, watching Sunny with a curious expression.

Stranger still was his choice of furniture. Not one of the couches. Not one of the chairs. But the cold, bare concrete.

Sunny's expression flickered, morphing between disdain and polite curiosity. The first was more accurate to his emotions, the second more amenable to his checkbook. "Mr. Johnson?" he said, trying to force a cheerful note into his tone.

The man sitting on the ground just crossed his arms. He peered up. "Often I get to speak with them," the man said.

Sunny shifted uncomfortably. "Sorry, what?

The man on the floor shook his head. "You're a strange breed. All of you." He waved a hand in a sort of dramatic flair. "There's no telling what you'll do. I watch, I wait, I listen. And I research. I'm good at finding things. I once found a Swiss Army knife in the middle of a pile of springs." He beamed fondly at the memory, shaking his head. He was still sitting on the concrete ground, as if it didn't bother him in the least.

Sunny shifted uncomfortably. "Were you the one I was speaking with on the phone yesterday?"

The man met his eyes and bobbed his head once. His eyes never left Sunny's face. There was something cold about that gaze. It reminded him of a crocodile he had once seen on a vacation to Florida.

The man on the floor just studied him and began tapping a long finger against his lips. "It's strange," he said in that faint, shuddering voice. "The sorts of things you remember, you know?"

He glanced off then smiled at some hidden thought. "I'm glad you came alone. I was hoping we could have a little word. What does it feel like to survive? When you know you killed someone?"

Sunny went stiff. He stared at the would-be tenant. "I beg your pardon?"

"Don't beg. Last guy tried. It doesn't work. But what does it feel like? I wish I could answer. But it's not the same."

Sunny had heard enough. The guy was some drug addict. Some weirdo. He didn't need to stand for this. "You should leave!" Sunny demanded.

The man on the ground pushed slowly to his feet, using his left hand. "I should. Soon. But you first."

"Umm, *no.* This isn't your place. We didn't reach terms. I'm telling you as the owner to get out."

The man smirked. White teeth flashed past curled lips. "You have rats, you know."

"No rats," he snapped. "Must be your imagination."

"It's just a few bucks," said the man. "So strange what people think of the value of life. You don't value others. But you value your own life, don't you? Is that fair?" He paused, cocking his head, then answered his own question. "I don't think it matters if it's fair. It just is. And so I value your life too, Mr. O'Leary. Long enough to have this little chat. I don't think there's anything you're going to tell me, though, that I want to hear."

Sunny could feel prickles up his spine now. This man was speaking in a way that made him very uncomfortable. He was ignoring the orders to leave. He spoke like someone in control. But he was just some stupid bum.

"I just want you to know," the man said, staring, "that this is going to be painless. It's the least I can do."

Sunny hesitated, opening his mouth to respond in confusion, but then the man suddenly began to move. One moment he had been standing against the wall, and the next he surged forward. Something appeared in his left hand.

Sunny stumbled back, trying to shout. The thing in his attacker's left hand swished, striking him across the head, *hard*.

Pain exploded. Stars danced across his vision. He tried to stand upright, but his legs caved under him. He tried to raise his hands to protect himself, but he didn't even know what he'd been hit with.

Faintly, panic flooding his system, he heard, as if from down a long tunnel, "And now we are going to do some *things*. It should be fun."

CHAPTER TWENTY ONE

Ilse sat in the dingy office space across from Mr. Lopez, her eyes studying his features. They were still stuck back at the scrapyard. She glanced at the clock over a smudged computer screen. Nearly two hours had passed since they'd first cuffed Lopez.

She glanced back towards the door, her eyes darting through the greasy windows in search of Agent Sawyer.

He still hadn't returned. She sighed, glancing at the clock again.

Tom had insisted he check out the scrapyard before they leave, searching for any point of entry Mr. Lopez might have used. Sawyer theorized the only reason Lopez had returned to the scene was to recover something he'd dropped—a weapon, evidence, DNA.

Ilse wasn't so sure, but she allowed Tom to take the lead. Plus, trapped alone in the dingy office space gave her a chance to speak with Lopez one on one without prying eyes or attentive ears.

Still... two hours was a long time to wait. As of yet, Tom clearly hadn't found anything.

This, more than anything, was beginning to trouble Ilse. She shifted uncomfortably in the rusty chair she'd borrowed. The furniture piece squeaked with her motion.

Why *had* Mr. Lopez returned to the junkyard? He'd gotten away with the kill... So why come back? Why be so cavalier—so... suspicious?

It was as if he'd *wanted* to get arrested.

Ilse's fingers tapped against the outline of her phone through her pocket. Part of her wanted to call Sawyer, to check on him. If he hadn't found some dropped weapon or speck of blood yet, she doubted he'd be able to in the dark.

Night was coming quickly, evening fading as it retreated from the moon's encroaching.

And yet the clock kept ticking. Sawyer remained missing, and Ilse was trapped in a room with a suspected serial killer, his hands cuffed to his own chair.

She studied the man, watching him. He refused to speak with her. At first, he'd given mumbled replies. But now, two hours in, he'd gone quiet, staring at the floor, his eyes misting occasionally. Something about the onset of night seemed to drain him.

Seasonal depressive disorder?

Some people had a potent mood shift with the descent of the sun.

Ilse shifted again, her chair creaking. She glanced towards the door a final time. Still no Sawyer.

No sense wasting the opportunity. She cleared her throat.

"I know what it is to lose someone," she said simply. Not normally a classic line of questioning for an FBI agent. But Ilse's training wasn't *only* found in a field manual.

He shifted in the chair, still not looking at her. "All three victims," she said faintly, "were people who'd harmed others due to negligence or egregious error. Matthew wasn't the only one."

She waited, studying Mr. Lopez. He was no longer smirking, no longer playing coy. He just looked sad. Depressed.

Was this the trigger? This descent into darkness? Was this why the killer so often struck at night.

She watched the way his left hand tensed, curling around the cuffs.

"Mr. Lopez," she said softly, "Why did you come back here? Why really?"

He looked up now, studying her. He shrugged.

"Please," she said. "I know you don't want to talk to me. But maybe I can help."

A bit of his old humor returned as his cheeks twitched up, but just as quickly he frowned again. "You can't help me," he murmured, breaking his latest, half-hour stretch of silence.

Ilse felt her heart skip, like a fisherman with a tug on her line. "Perhaps not. But I am trying to understand. Can you please help me?"

He shook his head. "I'm not quiet because I'm trying to hide anything," he said simply. "I'm quiet because I've told you everything. I didn't kill anyone. I came here to gloat. I wanted to see the place where that murderer was killed." He nodded adamantly. "I'm glad he's dead."

"You keep saying... but don't you see how that makes you look? You were angry at Matthew."

"Furious."

"You wanted him dead."

"Absolutely."

"You returned to the crime scene to see your work."

He shook his head. "Not my work," he said simply. "Believe me or not. I don't care. Penny got her justice—I don't have anything to prove to you." He sighed and stared at the ground again.

And once more, Ilse's stomach twisted.

He wasn't defending himself. Wasn't even trying to... He had all the markers of someone in control of their choices. But he didn't strike her as a sadist. He didn't have antisocial personality disorder, judging by how deeply he cared for his wife.

Sometimes, psychopaths could form particularly strong bonds with individuals. But Mr. Lopez had a capacity for empathy. It didn't fit.

What if he truly *was* telling the truth. But if so... That would mean...

Something suddenly pounded on the door. Ilse jolted, jerking upright. The door swung open, and Sawyer stood there, breathing heavily, gasping, his eyes wide.

Ilse stared at her partner. "Tom?" she said hesitantly.

He tried to speak but was too out of breath. He doubled over, hands on his knees, gasping at the ground and holding up a finger as if to ask for a moment. Once he calmed, he straightened again, breathing heavily.

"Come with me," he said simply.

Ilse blinked. "Wh—what about him?"

Sawyer shook his head. "It's not him."

"I—what?"

Sawyer shook his head more adamantly. "One of the cops will come up here. Keep him on trespassing. But it's not him, doc. He didn't kill them."

Ilse stared. "H-how can you be sure?"

"Because," Sawyer said. "He was cuffed to a fence for the last six hours. He was in our custody for two more hours."

"And?"

"And," Sawyer said, still breathing, "We found another body."

Ilse stared. "What? Where?"

Sawyer's jaw tightened his hand clenched at his side. He looked her dead in the eyes. "Here," he said. "We found another body *here*. More cops on their way—they're setting up roadblocks. Questioning anyone. Now come!"

He turned, leaving the door open and broke into a jog, hastening away again.

Ilse shot a confused look towards Mr. Lopez. He didn't even glance up. Never had she seen a depression settle so quickly like a lead blanket. Even his movements were slower now. He breathed softer. She stared at where he was cuffed to the chair.

Tom said a cop was on the way to babysit. Part of her thought to wait... But if Tom was telling the truth...

Shit. “Stay here!” she snapped. “Don't move!” She pushed to her feet, marched out of the office and glanced down the darkened hill.

She spotted the police officers from the sedan moving in their direction. She waved a hand, like a pale flag in the night. “He's here!” she called out, pointing. “Just in here!”

The officers marched steadily towards her, no urgency to their motions. Sawyer, on the other hand, was still jogging away, kicking up dust as he hastened deeper, further into the maze of old automobiles piled on each other, walls of rust and labyrinths of metal.

She waited a bit longer for the cops to draw nearer. But then, once they were in sight of the door, Mr. Lopez still sitting motionless, she turned, breaking into run after Sawyer and hurrying through the scrapyard.

***

Ilse stared at the metal freezer, toppled on its side. Black strands of duct tape had been wrapped around and around the freezer. A long, length of chain—the links shattered—scattered the dirt at the base of the freezer.

Sawyer was staring at the dusty ground, pointing towards impressions in the dirt. “He came from the south,” Sawyer muttered, “that way!”

Mr. Jerome, the old worker, followed Sawyer's gesture. He winced, staring down a hill, then nodded once. “The river,” he said simply.

Sawyer looked over. “What river?”

“Just what we call the smaller parts and pieces. It borders a fence along a dirt road. He must have come through the fence.”

Sawyer cursed, shaking his head. He glanced at the tracks. “Too small for a truck,” he said. “I think he's using an ATV and a hitch. At least this time. Dammit!” Sawyer cursed, slapping a hand against his thigh. “How didn't we see him?”

Ilse had the answer for this. All around them, old shipping containers created a wall blocking any view. Even sounds were deflected, echoing off the tinny, metal surfaces.

While Sawyer had been scrounging around the previous crime scene, and Ilse had been in the office with Mr. Lopez, the actual killer had snuck up from the back part of the expansive junkyard, dropped off his latest creation, then left.

Without so much as making a sound.

They'd been tricked.

More accurately, they'd tricked themselves.

Ilse felt her frustration turn to sheer anger. She didn't like feeling stupid. Didn't like being duped. But the evidence was in the open, metal freezer compartment. The strands of duct tape had been cut by Mr. Jerome and a utility knife.

Sawyer was stalking up the path, following the trail. Behind them, up the hill, back near the entrance and the office, Ilse could hear voices. Paramedics had arrived, most likely. The cops would direct them. But it would take some time for them to move through the junkyard maze.

Ilse stared at the side of the metal freezer.

Streaks of blood down the edge. That's what had alerted Jerome on his rounds.

She sighed. "Sawyer, where were you?" she said.

Tom glanced back at her, hands on his hips. He sighed. "Over by the first crime scene. It's past the shipping containers, past a stack of trucks... I didn't hear anything. *Nothing.*" He gritted his teeth in fury and slammed his fist against his leg.

He turned back towards the victim inside the freezer.

Ilse's own gaze was once again drawn to him as well.

An older man, with wispy hair, also caked in blood. He'd been asphyxiated. Left to die of oxygen deprivation in the box. The cause of death wasn't confirmed, but the bluish tinge of his lips, the lack of any other injuries besides the apparent head wound, and the nature of the container seemed clear enough.

Someone had locked him alive inside the freezer, duct-taped all the air passages and allowed him to die from lack of oxygen.

"Do—do you think it's the same guy?" Ilse asked, shivering at the thought of two killers. "Did he know we were here? Why come back?"

Sawyer shook his head. "Convenience. It worked the last time." Tom cursed, rubbing his head. "Dammit, Ilse. He's mocking us. He dropped a body at a site with two FBI agents and two cops. He's playing now. *Playing.*"

Ilse bit her lip. She didn't disagree. Tom was right.

They were being mocked. And worst of all, another body was dropped.

"Any chance of that ID?" Ilse asked, glancing towards Sawyer.

Tom sighed, reaching for the wallet he'd found and placed on the hood of the old car next to him. He'd already called in the identification. “They'll get back soon,” Tom said. “And no, I'm not calling Rudiger this time. I'm not in the mood.”

Ilse felt similarly. She watched as Sawyer studied the tracks in the dirt again. “Generic tread,” he was muttering. “Dammit!” he slapped his leg again. He glanced at her.

Normally, her partner wasn't nearly so expressive. But whatever was bubbling beneath the surface with Tom was quickly boiling over. Still, Ilse couldn't focus on both Sawyer's troubles and their case.

Not to mention the parole hearing still at the top of her mind.

She shifted, feeling a twinge along her spine from their car crash. As she moved, her eyes were caught by something strange about the freezer lid.

She frowned, stepping closer and studying a strap of yellow cord wrapped around the lid's handle.

The cord extended down, dangling towards the open compartment. When closed, though, the cord would have served no purpose. She frowned, staring at this oddly placed piece of rope.

The handle was a wide one. The lid for the freezer very heavy. The cord would have made it easier to reach...

Odd.

Frowning to herself, Ilse reached across the top of the freezer, careful not to lean too far over and determined not to stare at the body. She pulled her sweater over her hand to touch the freezer's handle, careful only to press against a portion of the rope in order not to disturb fingerprints.

She could reach the handle, but it would take more force than she could manage to close it one-handed. She reached out with her other hand, then, grunting, she managed to shift the lead, closing it slightly.

The yellow cord swung as she did. She stared at it, confused. A strange thing to catch her attention, but something about the cord just... it didn't make sense.

She pushed the freezer lid open again and stared into the compartment once more towards the blue-tinged face.

The coroner would have an official report by tomorrow morning. But even the coroner was running late.

“Doc!” Sawyer called out, gesturing at her. “We have a positive ID!”

Ilse double-checked the lid was still up and then she broke into a jog, hurrying towards where Sawyer was standing in a dirt path, peering down the hill towards more and more refuse as far either of them could see. The operation was an expansive one. At the bottom of the hill, she spotted a rusted fence post. But no actual mesh wiring.

Sawyer pointed. “He came that way. I bet that's how he got in the first time. Even if they'd had cameras, they wouldn't have seen him.”

Ilse nodded. “Cautious, isn't he?”

Sawyer hesitated. “In a way. Here's our guy. Sunny O'Leary.” Sawyer turned his phone so she could see the screen. Tom added, “You really should get one of these, you know. Rawley is gonna give you trouble if you don't.”

Ilse smiled sweetly, patting Sawyer on the arm. “And I'm so very grateful you cover for me, so I don't have to subject myself to one of those infernal devices.”

Sawyer snorted. He scrolled on his phone, mutter, “Early fifties. Lives local.” Sawyer paused, whistling. “Nice bank account. Looks like he makes most of his money from real estate.”

Ilse glanced back towards the metal coffin. “He's a landlord?”

“Was... huh, not a very good one.”

Ilse looked back. “Why's that?”

“We have a few complaints. I'm... I'm not seeing any accidents, though,” Sawyer said with a frown.

“Car crashes? Do you have insurance claims?”

Sawyer circled to another page, then grunted. “Yeah—nothing significant. A fender bender about a decade ago. That's it.”

Ilse studied the screen. “What were those reports about him being a bad landlord?”

“Oh, you know, the usual. Neglect. Not fixing things on time.” Sawyer circled back again, leaning in so Ilse could see better. The bright glow from the screen illuminated their faces and reflected off the corrugated metal wall flanking them.

“Not fixing things?” Ilse wrinkled her nose. “Doesn't exactly fit our MO. Was anyone hurt on his properties?”

Sawyer paused but shook his head. “Nothing reported at least. But... well, huh...”

“What?”

“The prices on these places. They're low. Like *really* low.”

Ilse frowned. “Think you could pull up a listing for one?”

Sawyer nodded, circling to the web browser app and entering one of the addresses from the assets sheet. After a few moments of spotty connection, a series of images loaded.

Sawyer whistled. “Shit—whoever took the photos tried their best, but I can see mold in like two of these.”

Ilse studied the image. “So he owns a bunch of cheap units in disrepair. Means poor tenants.”

“Probably.”

Ilse was still frowning. “Poor tenants might not have been able to sue him even if they wanted to.”

Sawyer looked up. “You think he caused an accident that was never reported?”

Ilse shrugged, turning back to the metal freezer. “Possibly. I don't know. But if so, how does the killer know that? How did he find out?”

Sawyer and Ilse stood next to each other in the dark of night, both staring towards their most recent victim. The sound of voices up the hill was now descending and figures moved down the dusty trail towards Sawyer and Ilse.

“Looks like paramedics are here,” Sawyer muttered.

Ilse just shook her head, feeling a deep, unsettling sense of discontent. Another dead end. What if this newest victim wasn't even murdered by the same killer? He was posed in something metal... but no brutalization of the skin. Except the head wound. That matched. The dump site matched. The caution matched...

But what if Mr. Lopez *was* their killer. And this was just an unlucky accident that a new body was dropped?

Her eyes darted back to the yellow cord dangling over the freezer. Something about it still bothered her, niggled at her mind. But what?

She felt her frustration mounting. They were missing something. Mr. Lopez didn't strike her as guilty. But her intuitions had been off in the past. Sawyer went by gut-instinct. She liked to have a bit more behind her decisions.

Still... what were the odds of this being a second killer?

She wrinkled her nose even as she said it and even gave a faint shake of her head. No... No that didn't make sense. Too many coincidences. The real killer was out there. Toying with them. He'd killed four people so far. Who was the fifth?

There would be a fifth. She knew that much. There was no reason for him to stop now. None of the victims were connected to each other except in the way they'd died and the accidents they'd caused. The landlord, though, it wasn't so clear.

She let out a puff of air.

“I—think—umm... think you can walk the paramedics through?”

she said.

"Sure. You going somewhere?"

"Just gonna get some air. I'll be back," she muttered.

Ilse turned, picking up her pace and moving away from the crime scene, between the shipping containers, stepping through shadows. There was something comforting about the dark. Something familiar.

She liked the dark. It helped her think. Her body still ached when she moved, and she winced as she did. The bruises, she imagined, would last for a while.

A fifth victim was inevitable. And worse still, they were no closer to finding the killer. A tentative connection among the victims he chose didn't help find the next candidate.

And it certainly didn't find the perpetrator.

They were at the deadest of ends.

And thinks were only looking bleaker.

Ilse picked up her pace, feeling Sawyer watching her. She needed some insight... needed... *something.* She fished her phone from her pocket, moving through the junkyard as fast as she could go.

She held her phone firmly like a lifeline but didn't lift it until she was out of sight, turning past one of the containers and fading into the dark.

CHAPTER TWENTY TWO

Ilse leaned against the metal shipping container, breathing heavily and trying to calm herself. The lack of sleep, the stress from the case, the ache from her bruises, the impending parole hearing... it was all getting to be too much.

But she'd trained for moments like these. She started with diaphragm breathing, in, out, slowly. As she did, she closed her eyes, allowing herself to experience the emotions of frustration, sadness, disappointment, anger.

Feeling was required. It was only *through* the pain she could reach resolution.

Her fingers still tremored against her phone. A physical reaction to stress. Nothing to do about it. If she calmed, her hand would. But one thing at a time.

She opened her eyes now, staring into the dark. The wind made a strange whistling sound as it blew across the surrounding corrugated metal containers. She wanted Sawyer to get help because she knew the best way to deal with demons was in community. With others.

She always tried to take that very advice herself.

And now, she dialed the number of her very own demon-killer.

He answered on the second ring. A friendly, warm tone, despite the late hour. “Becks!” Dr. Mitchell said. “It's absolutely wonderful to hear from you—it's been too long!”

She paused, smiling and picturing her old mentor's twinkling blue eyes and Santa Claus bushy beard. Mitchell was a health nut who biked everywhere and, despite his prosthetic arm, he never allowed his injury to hold him back from being one of the most sought after professionals in the business.

Now, even just hearing his voice, the warmth, some of her emotions began to calm. Some of the stress faded. The bruises didn't subside, but the mental effect of the aches lessened.

“Hey Donovan,” she said. “How—er, how are you?”

“Fine, doing fine. Working on the new book. But it's slow going,” he chuckled. “I’m sure you remember your dissertation.”

“Yeah. Yes of course,” she said. She closed her eyes again, just inhaling, breathing slowly. She knew the difference between vulnerability and transparency, though it had taken her a long time to learn it. In one version, someone's flaws and ills were used as simple information, a shield of sorts. In the other, it opened her up to potentially being hurt.

But she trusted Mitchell, more than anyone.

"I—I'm working a case," she said.

"Oh—yes! How is the new career going?"

"Umm, fine. I guess. This one's rough, you know. We... we work with them *after.* With the survivors." She let out a shuddering sigh. "I don't know how to work with the ones we lose... Don't know how to help them."

She thought of the corpse in the freezer back down the path. Shivered as she pictured the landlord's blue-tinged skin.

"I'm sorry to hear that, Becks," Mitchell replied. "Anything I can do?"

"Umm... No, not really." She forced a little chuckle. "My—my dad's parole hearing is coming up." Even as she said it, she felt her stomach twist. Not even Mitchell knew the extent of her family history. He didn't know her name wasn't really Ilse Beck. Didn't know much about her before she'd found him as a teenager. He didn't pry—didn't care to ask. He certainly didn't know *everything* about her father. But he was good at his job and had gleaned enough over the course of years.

Instead of prying for further information, he simply said, "And how are you doing with that news?"

"I... well, not great. Not great. I want to be there."

"Really? Why?"

She sighed, puffing air. This was the sort of question where she could choose to be vulnerable or to hide. It hurt to choose the former, but it inevitably, always helped more than pretense. She sighed and said, "I'm scared... Scared of what he did. What he might do. I don't know if he deserves to be let loose. But... I also help people all the time who've been hurt. I try to understand, to be compassionate..." She trailed off and shook her head, her hair swishing lightly against the metal wall at her back. "I guess... closure. I don't know that I'd sleep knowing he was out there."

Mitchell just listened, waiting for her to finish. Then he said, "You know, when I lost my arm—I know I've told you the story—but when I lost it, I spent nearly a month waiting for it to regrow." He laughed.

"Like a lizard, I guess. It was just too painful to think it was *gone.* Permanently gone." He sighed but said, "Over the years, I've come to realize sometimes we don't need to replace the things we've lost. We just need to grieve them. The fear of loss grows most potent when we don't allow ourselves to *feel* the hurt."

"I—I'm not sure I know what you mean."

"I mean, Ilse, your childhood was taken from you. It can't be replaced. It can be grieved. It should be. Sometimes, if tended properly, the trees that grow the tallest are the ones that are replanted, moved to better soil. In the transplant process, branches can break, twigs fall off. Things are lost... But then it grows. It becomes something more. The giant oak doesn't miss its fallen twigs."

Ilse hesitated, letting out another sigh. "I don't quite know what that means, but it sounds nice, Mitchell. I appreciate you taking the time." She smiled. "I'll try to grieve my fallen twigs."

Mitchell chuckled. "Ha... I guess it does sound a little pretentious."

"No! No! Not at all. I just... I'm not as smart as you."

"Ha!" Donovan laughed. "We both know that's not true."

Silence lingered for a moment. Normally, someone might take the opportunity to end the call. But Mitchell didn't. He allowed the silence to linger, the space to stretch. He allowed Ilse to stay on the line with him without rushing her off.

She loved him for it. And for other things.

As she thought of her mentor, of his words, her brow furrowed. Some things that were lost couldn't be replaced. She thought back to that crime-scene with the welded door. Only the left door. Thought to the little yellow cord above the freezer. A cord to help close the lid... That was its obvious use. Ilse needed to use both her hands to close it... It hadn't been *too* difficult.

So why the extension cord? Why the left side of the door?

Unless...

Her eyes widened.

Left-handed. Dr. Mitchell had lost an arm. The killer was left-handed.

"Shit," she said. "Sorry. I—I have to go. Thank you!"

"Goodnight, Ilse. Don't hesitate to call if you need anything. I'll keep my phone on and by the bed tonight."

She smiled at this. "Thanks! Bye!"

But as he bid his farewell, her heart was already pattering. She closed her phone, her skin buzzing.

Not left-handed.
One handed.
The killer was missing a limb.

CHAPTER TWENTY THREE

It had been quite a while since the survivor had purchased a car. He felt somewhat out of place strolling the used car lot, moving under the cover of night between flashy metal. Ahead, through a blue window, he spotted a single light beaming out into the dark parking lot outside the dealership.

He smiled at the light, tapping his one good hand against his leg. The other arm cocked slightly, crooked at the elbow. Most of the arm was missing past the elbow. He'd never gotten around to buying a prosthetic—didn't have the money. Didn't really trust them, anyway, especially not the mechanical type.

He watched through the window ahead as shadows moved about inside the building. A lonely, solitary figure. The survivor turned to study the vehicles, his eyes narrowing as he did. Normally, he liked to create his monuments back home and bring them to the site.

But things had changed...

He'd nearly stumbled on the feds—it had been sheer dumb luck no one had heard him dropping off the most recent tragedy. The silver freezer had been heavy to begin with. The scraping sound of friction had almost drawn the wrong attention.

He'd spotted the cops in time, though. They'd been busy studying the previous crime scene.

Of course, he'd managed to make good his getaway and now...

Now he was on the hunt again.

He had the taste for it now. And my, oh my, how many objects of affection had he found? A quick search or two on the internet, and a little bit of due diligence, and he was able to narrow down the field quite nicely.

This newest wannabe survivor was going to be the next step in his creations. A monument in motion. A monument in light.

"Did you bring it?" he muttered to himself.

He nodded at his own question, slipping his good hand into his oversized pocket and pulling out a small can of lighter fluid. He scanned the late-night parking lot once more, searching for the perfect candidate.

Immolation. An odd word. But he'd read it in an article about this particular survivor. The dealership owner had sold a lemon to an older lady the previous year. He'd guaranteed the integrity of the vehicle. But it came out in a later lawsuit that Sanjey Rydel had *known* he sold a lemon with a perforated gas tank.

They hadn't been able to prove anything beyond a reasonable doubt. But the court records were clear.

The survivor sighed faintly, swishing the bottle of lighter fluid and listening to the pleasant sound.

"Do you think he'll scream?" he whispered to himself, watching the shadow through the blinds. "Does fire wake them?" He paused, considering this, but then shook his head. "No—no, just hit him hard enough. It'll be fine." He paused again, shifting uncomfortably.

At last, his eyes landed on a big, black SUV with a giant helium balloon hovering above the left mirror. Perfect.

He smirked and stalked towards the SUV, using his dexterous hand to uncap the lighter fluid while bracing the bottle against his chest with his other arm. The pungent scent reached his nostrils soon enough, and he tilted the container, watching as a faint stream of liquid spilled onto the SUV. Anointing oil for his monument.

Once he'd slicked the whole thing, he approached the nearest window.

A flashing red light pulsed from the dash. The alarm was engaged. Perfect.

He let out a shaking little sigh, thinking back to his own horrible accident. A blinking red light had been broken *then.* He hadn't known the machine was operating. The mechanic had left the repair job until morning after an all-night bender. He'd preferred to drink himself into a stupor rather than protect his coworkers.

The survivor scowled, remembering the mechanic's God-awful face. Small things compiled. Snowballs tumbled. Just a *small* thing. A pinkie finger. A toe. A hand. Small. The survivor had lost a hand because of negligence. Lost his job. Lost his house. His wife had left him. Taken the kid. The boyfriend of the wife had killed the kid in a drunken stupor. Such small, small things.

Even as he considered it, his emotions were faded. He didn't think too long on them. A little bitty snowball tumbling, tumbling...

And the man who'd committed the small error?

The negligent mechanic had gone and died in a car crash before the survivor could do anything about it.

The bastard had taken his hand, his job, his wife, his kid, his *everything* and also his vengeance.

So... so he'd found others.

Other substitutes just like the mechanic who'd maimed him. Others who deserved to go the same way.

He stared at the SUV slicked with lighter fluid. Half the bottle still remained. These damn machines... people relied too much on machines. Reckless people. Weak people. They endangered their own lives and the lives of others by partnering with these mechanical monstrosities.

They were resurrecting monsters without even knowing it.

He felt another flash of phantom pain and snarled, raising his elbow suddenly and slamming it into the SUV's window.

The glass shattered. The alarm started trilling.

He took the rest of the open bottle of lighter fluid and dumped it on the front seat. He then tossed the bottle into the car as well.

The shrill alarm continued to yodel, but he didn't mind. He'd heard worse from louder before. Especially at his old job. Now, he had a new vocation.

Self-employed, really.

He turned, once again facing the window with the only light in the car dealership. The shadow he'd spotted earlier was moving frantically, hastening towards the door to investigate the sound.

Perfect.

The survivor smirked, leaning back against the hood of the car and waiting patiently. The scent of lighter fluid lingered in his nose and the alarm continued to blare.

CHAPTER TWENTY FOUR

Ilse hastened up the hill, moving back between the shipping containers, her footsteps hurried, her breath coming in pants. She rushed towards where Sawyer was speaking with the paramedics who had already loaded the corpse onto the stretcher judging by the lump beneath a white sheet circled with black straps.

Sawyer looked up, frowning, his face illuminated thanks to the lapel flashlights on the paramedics. He noticed Ilse's urgent movements and turned away from the man he was talking to in order to face her.

"Tom," she said breathlessly, still half-jogging, half-striding. "I think I know who we're looking for."

Sawyer ignored the paramedics completely now, still frowning, and took a couple of steps towards her. "You good, doc?"

She shook her head. "I—look, Tom, I think the killer is left-handed because..." she swallowed, gathering her breath, thinking through the theory. Her eyes darted back towards the simple yellow cord dangling from the freezer handle. She thought of the welded door.

It made sense. She knew it did.

She nodded, summoning her courage, and pressed on. "I—I think our killer is missing an arm." As she said it out loud, she knew how it sounded. She winced in anticipation of an eye roll or a snort of humor.

But Sawyer just watched her, dead-serious.

"Why?"

She pointed towards the freezer. "Look at that yellow cord. It's an extender for the handle. It's new, compared to how old the freezer is. It means the killer put it there."

Sawyer looked and shrugged. "So?"

"So," she said, "why go to the trouble of accessorizing a murder box?"

"Maybe he used it before he dumped it."

"Possibly, but even then, it doesn't take any effort to close the freezer with both hands. I tried it. But one handed? I tried that also..." She shook her head. "On its own, it's just a stupid yellow cord. But it's not on its own. The coroner told us he was left-handed. That's rare."

"Sure, but less rare than *one-handed.*"

She nodded quickly. "I—I know. But remember Matthew's car? The welded door? He only welded the left side."

"Sure... maybe he was just lazy?"

Ilse refused to concede yet. She kept pressing on. "Did you notice the train-track monument? He dismembered the body. And placed all the pieces in those metal loops..." She wrinkled her nose in disgust.

But Sawyer stared at her. "All the pieces were there... except for the right hand."

"Exactly!" she said. "The right hand was missing. I know it's not a solid lead. But... but it's *something.* I've been wondering why the killer—who is clearly a sadist—knocks them out first. It almost seems, you know, merciful."

Sawyer was no longer objecting; his green eyes had narrowed, and he stared at her. "So we're definitely not going with the Lopez theory..."

"Definitely."

Sawyer glanced back at the stretcher and the white blanket, then returned his attention to Ilse. He sighed. "I see. Well, doc, *why* is he showing them mercy first?"

"I don't think it's mercy. I think he's scared of being overpowered. If he only has one hand, he knocks them unconscious in order to do what he wants with them without resistance. It isn't compassion, it's necessity. He's not strong enough to torture them while they're conscious."

"Shit. That's dark."

Ilse shrugged. "It fits."

Sawyer was tapping his lips with a long finger. "One-handed scrapyard killer, huh? Someone familiar with the junkyards. Familiar with the terrain, the security. Someone who can work with metal in a pinch... We know someone like that, don't we?"

Ilse was already nodding. She exhaled shakily. This was the reason she'd jogged back. The urgency was returning once again. She winced. "Ian's brother—the third victim. He had one of the workers with him, trying to console him. The scrapyard worker only—"

"Had one damn arm," Sawyer returned, staring at her. "Shit, Ilse... It's him. That scrapyard worker back at the third crime scene. He knows the scrapyards. Knows the businesses inside and out. He's one-handed, just like you said. He was at the crime scene with us. He knew we didn't have shit. That's why he's been so bold!"

Ilse was nodding eagerly. It wasn't a perfect fit. She knew that. Sawyer did too. But with this newest body, Lopez had a perfect alibi.

Without him, they had no other suspects.

The one-armed theory was a bold one. But the more she thought about it, the more she considered the many pieces, it all made sense. No single proof was there. But the cumulative case of small proofs compounded into a giant ball of evidence.

Sawyer was already, turning, fishing his phone from his pocket. "Come on, doc—we need his address."

"What about that gate guard of yours!" Ilse called out, hastening after him. The two of them kicked up dust as they hustled past the bewildered paramedics.

"Yeah—yeah good call." Sawyer pressed his phone to his cheek, his eyes still narrowed, his breath coming quickly. Together, the two of them climbed back up the slope, moving rapidly towards where they'd parked.

***

Ilse winced as their vehicle screeched to a halt outside the address Tom's contact had provided. It hadn't taken much, either. Just a bit of chatting about a potential NBA expansion team in Seattle and the promise of some beers. The gate guard had sung like a canary.

Ilse and Sawyer had confirmed the address. And now the two of them hastened up the concrete path towards the door of the small townhouse. The left half of the multi-family arrangement faced a wooded lot behind an old shopping center with limited traffic. A quiet, babbling stream poured from a marble fountain, down to a rocky bed, along a landscaped yard and through a bed of purple flowers in bloom.

The porch light illuminated the agents as they hastened up the steps. Night gave them some cover. Most neighbors were sleeping now. The lights doused in their homes, the streets mostly empty. No one was walking their dog.

Ilse felt an eerie chill along her back as she placed herself on one side of the door, opposite Sawyer, allowing him to go first, as was often their arrangement in the more physically taxing scenarios.

Sawyer gave her a look, raising an eyebrow. She flashed a thumbs up.

Sawyer knocked on the door, loudly. "FBI!" he called. "Mike Eton, open up!" He hit the door again, his jaw clenched.

Ilse tensed by the window. She spotted the purple and lace fabric shift. An eye pressed to the glass. Then, she thought she heard a faint sigh.

The door *clicked.* A chain rattled as the door was pushed a few inches forward. The same eye from behind the curtains now appeared in the slit in the door. It roamed, glancing between the agents. “Yes?” a sleepy voice demanded.

Ilse recognized the man. He was no longer wearing overalls or worker's gloves. Now, he wore smooth, cotton pajamas. They looked comfortable, just like the fluffy, bunny-rabbit shaped slippers. Inside, past him, she glimpsed a neat, well-kept home. She even detected a fragrance as if from a candle warmer exuding out into the night.

Mr. Eton's beard was trimmed, his hair disheveled but apparently hastily combed judging by the way the bangs were parted. This was a man who cared about appearances. Who cared about spectacle.

He was also missing his right hand. Ilse could see it from where she stood. His arm braced against the door, but his sleeve was cut off, tied in a knot around the stump. Eton was continuing to frown at them.

“Sir,” Sawyer said firmly, “Please open the door; we need to speak with you.”

The man shifted uncomfortably, leaving the chain in place. “What's this about?”

“Open up!” Sawyer demanded. “FBI!”

“I heard you the first time,” came the irritated reply. “Say, don't I recognize you two? Weren't you the ones back at...” He winced, wrinkling his nose. “Great,” he said, sighing. “Look, it's been a long day for me, too. Can't this wait until morning?”

“Sir,” Sawyer said more insistently. “Open the door *now* or I'm going to arrest you.”

Michael Eton blinked, staring through the crack in his door. He swallowed faintly, his Adam's apple bouncing. “Oh...” he muttered.

Sawyer shot Ilse a quick look, and muttered, "Do we have confirmation?"

Ilse gave a quick shake of her head. She glanced back towards Michael, who was frowning at them. "Confirmation?" he said, a note of panic rising in his voice. "What do you think I did?"

Ilse didn't reply. She did move her hand, though, touching against her phone. They had placed a request with forensics to confirm the theory about a one-handed killer. It would take time to get any affirmation from the coroner. Due to the nature of the killings, and the location, two separate clinics were being used.

She gave a faint shake of her head toward Sawyer. No confirmation yet.

But she knew what she'd seen. It fit. Michael had even been at the crime scene. It had been staring them in the face all along.

"Look," Michael said hesitantly, trying to close the door. "Maybe you guys should speak with my lawyer."

Tom caught the frame with his foot. He reached out, rattling the chains still holding it closed. "You need to open the door. Now."

But Mr. Eton was panicking. His eyes widened. He exhaled softly. Ilse heard the soft sound of a little bell behind him. She glanced past the man to see a fluffy, white poodle prancing into the room.

One look at the strangers in the door, and the poodle began to bark. This sound only further seemed to exacerbate Michael's anxiety. Now he was shifting and twisting in place. His pajamas displayed sweat stains beneath the arms.

"You have no right," he said, his voice shaking. "I'm a taxpayer. A citizen. You have no right! This is my home! Go away!"

He tried to shove the door.

Ilse could hear more barking. The light from the townhouse on the other side of the structure turned on. She heard voices coming from the neighbors' place.

Tom could hear them too, and his eyes narrowed in frustration. "Don't make this difficult on yourself," Sawyer reprimanded.

But Mr. Eton had already made up his mind. He kept trying to shove the door. Now he was shouting. "Attack!" he screamed. "They're trying to kidnap me!"

Sawyer growled. "I'm warning you."

But it didn't seem to matter. Michael was beyond threats. Beyond consoling. The dog behind him continued to yap and yowl.

Sawyer had enough. Ilse could see the way he'd tensed. Noticed him leaned back for a second and then he brought his body weight slamming into the door.

Michael stumbled back, shouting. Without the added barrier, Sawyer backed off again and kicked as hard as he could. The small chain holding the door shattered.

Ilse exhaled a deep sigh as Sawyer thundered into the room. "Hands where I can see them!" he shouted.

Ilse followed closely behind.

Michael was on the ground, sobbing and shaking his head. He tried to hold them back, his only hand raised against them.

Ilse stared at where he kicked and where he struggled. Right now, he looked so helpless. Defenseless. Her heart spasmed. But she had to remind herself about the crime scenes. Had to remember what she'd seen the killer do. What she had seen Michael do. No, this was an act.

He was shifting on the carpet now, still sobbing.

Ilse gestured at Tom. "Cuffs," she called.

Sawyer was busy trying to wrangle Mr. Eton. He hesitated, reaching back for the handcuffs, but then pausing. He winced. "How?" he muttered.

In the end, Sawyer ended up cuffing the man's hand behind his back to the hem of his pajama bottoms.

"That's cashmere!" he protested.

But Tom wasn't paying attention; he dragged Michael to his feet. The little poodle kept howling.

Ilse winced. The whole neighborhood had probably woken up at this point.

Heads low, Ilse and Tom pushed Mr. Eton from his house.

As they left, Ilse glanced around the place. So clean. So neat. Perfectly maintained. Not a dish out of place. Was he playing them? Was he really the sadistic killer she thought?

He had to be.

It all fit.

But that meant he was an incredible actor. She would have to be on the top of her game to get a confession this time.

Ilse and Sawyer hastened towards their car, leading Michael in front of them.

"Someone needs to feed Nibbles!" Michael shouted over his shoulder towards his neighbors' house. "Only half a cup. Please. Dear God, feed Nibbles!"

"Famous last words," Sawyer muttered as he pushed Michael into the back of the car. And then hastened towards the driver's side.

CHAPTER TWENTY FIVE

Ilse stared at her phone, reading the message as she sat in the interrogation room. Sawyer kept glancing sidelong at her, trying to get glances of the message as well.

Ilse felt a flicker of relief as she finished the text. The coroner's office had confirmed. Forensics agreed. A one-handed killer. It wasn't guaranteed but it seemed very probable.

Ilse's heart fluttered with a sense of vindication.

She stared at Michael. The man was still in his pajamas. Mercifully, he had been uncuffed. His only good hand rested on the table. His other was hidden out of sight behind a knotted sleeve.

Sawyer was in his usual place, walking back and forth by the door. Every so often, he shot a glance towards Mr. Eton, frowning as he did.

Ilse studied the person across from her.

He looked like a lost little lamb—his voice was soft, his tone indignant. He was shaking his head with fervor. "You have the wrong guy!" he said, pleading. "This has to be some kind of joke—look at me!"

He raised his injured arm and dropped it again.

"Where were you the last three nights?" Sawyer said. "We already know you were at the third crime scene."

"I *work* there. I didn't have a choice."

"Where were you?

"When?"

"At night Monday through tonight. Tell me."

He just shook his head. "I live alone. You saw that. Nibbles can vouch for me."

Ilse shook her head. "Now isn't the time for jokes, Mr. Eton. We want to know if you have an alibi for the night of the murder."

He looked astonished, shaking his head. "I don't know what to tell you. I keep saying I'm not a murderer. What makes you think I would—"

"Why is your phone encrypted?" Tom circled the table, like a shark eyeing a surfboard.

Michael looked uncomfortable at this question. "Is there some rule against technological safety?"

"It's military grade encryption," Tom said. "But you have no ties."

Michael rubbed at the bridge of his nose. "I just got it from a friend. He's trying out some new software."

Ilse leaned in. "What do you have in your phone that's worth protecting? Or... hiding?"

He snorted and leaned back. "I don't have to tell you that. You have nothing."

Ilse raised her phone. "I have input from forensics that say the killer was one-handed. How many one-handed scrapyard employees do you think there are?"

He shifted nervously. "How the hell should I know? Besides, I don't even work in the yards. I work in the offices. I'm just there for itineraries and inventory."

"Administration," Tom said. "So you would know the exact times the shifts changed."

Michael sighed in exasperation. "It's a coincidence."

"And you're saying you have no alibi for any of the nights of the murders?"

"I don't go out. I prefer staying indoors. That's not a crime. It's called introversion."

His tone was exasperated, his hand gesticulating wildly. Every time he punctuated a sentence, his voice would go an octave higher. Ilse wasn't sure what to make of this. On one hand, he fit the bill. He had means, opportunity, though the motive still wasn't clear.

"What happened to your arm?" She nodded at the injury.

"I beg your pardon?"

"Your arm. What happened to it?"

"A birth defect," he retorted. "I've only ever had one arm. Thank you so much for bringing it up."

Ilse shook her head. "Our killer only has one arm. You have to see how this looks."

He just glared at her.

Sawyer said, "If you're just gonna sit there lying to us, there's no point in continuing this—you have no alibi. You work at the crime scenes. You just admitted that you knew everyone's schedule, so you could slip in and out to put up your ghastly monuments."

"No monuments. I had no *monuments*." Again, he hit a higher octave.

Ilse shifted uncomfortably in her seat. It all fit perfectly. And yet she felt uneasy. His apartment had just been so clean. Neat. Everything perfectly arranged. Ordered. She knew that feeling. That need for order and organization.

She would never diagnose someone as obsessive-compulsive based on a clean room. But everything about his presentation... even his job in administration...

So why did that bother her?

It took her second to realize why. But the crime scenes had been messy. Even the train track monument had been disorderly. Horrible protrusions every which way. No symmetry. The freezer had been placed next to rectangular storage containers. But it had been placed lengthwise. Not parallel.

A stupid thing. But these were the sorts of things she was paid to pay attention to.

Besides, as she studied Michael across the table, something else occurred to her.

If he was telling the truth about his arm, that it had been a birth defect from childhood, then the theory wouldn't work. What motive would he have to target the survivors of accidents? There was no correlation. No connection.

She could feel her heartbeat quickening.

What was she missing?

It had to be something obvious.

"Look, maybe you can talk to some of my neighbors," Michael was saying hopefully, "I'm sure one of them must've seen me. Then again, I do tend to stay inside and watch TV mostly. I don't walk Nibbles until late. But you have to believe me. You have the wrong guy."

Ilse felt another jolt of uncertainty. There he went again. Earnest, genuine. Almost too perfect. As if he had rehearsed these lines. And why was his phone encrypted? He had refused to give them the passcode. What was he hiding? Videos of his murders? Images of the victims' addresses? Plans for the monuments?

It fit, but not perfectly. Michael was clearly clever. Far smarter than someone would expect from a junkyard employee.

Often, obsessive-compulsive tendency hinted at other, more severe mental issues.

In her case it looked like trauma and anxiety.

Was this man a narcissistic killer? Was she just losing her edge?

She pushed slowly to her feet, still studying Michael.

"Tom, you can take it for a moment," she muttered.

Sawyer just shrugged, flashed a thumbs up.

She moved quickly, hurrying to the door and pushing out.

She just wasn't sure. She'd been confident in the theory. She was still confident in the theory. The killer was one-handed but was it Michael Eton?

That was the question.

She just had to dig a little deeper on her own.

She pushed through the interrogation room door, out into the hall, allowing it to swing shut behind her as Sawyer launched into a line of questioning of his own.

CHAPTER TWENTY SIX

Ilse paced the hallway outside the interrogation room, doing her best to focus on her call. Sawyer's voice came muffled through the closed metal door as Tom continued to interrogate their suspect in hopes of a slip-up or a confession.

Ilse still couldn't be sure. Either they were being played by a master manipulator, or they'd jumped the gun.

She listened to the voice on her phone, still pacing.

"Darling, I'm looking," Rudiger said, "but I don't see any insurance claims for missing appendages in the local scrapyards. Nothing in disability filing. Nothing in accident reports. No charges. No lawsuits... I'm even checking hospital reports—nothing..."

Ilse sighed, pausing by the same vending machine Sawyer had assaulted the last time. She stared at the bag of chips which was still lodged in the top portion.

"Thanks, Rudiger," she said. "What about that other thing I asked?"

"Oh—yes, our new would-be culprit. Well, he was telling you the truth, dear. He's been missing that arm of his since he was born."

Ilse winced, feeling her stomach twist. "So it really is a genetic defect?" she whispered. "Not the result of some accident? Some negligence?"

"I'm afraid not. I have a couple of social media posts from his mother I'm looking at right now. Buncha old pictures when he was a toddler."

Ilse sighed. If their suspect was telling the truth about the source of his missing arm, it weakened his connection to the case. The killer was targeting people involved in accidents. Survivors who had been negligent and caused someone else harm. But now it didn't fit their scrapyard employee in the other room.

She paced back across the hall, listening as Sawyer continued questioning their man.

She paused by the door, staring at a shadow moving beneath it which suggested Sawyer was also growing restless.

"Dammit," she muttered.

"You're so cute when you swear," Rudiger declared.

Ilse smirked. "Anyone else, Rudy, and that might be harassment."

"No, no, dear. I compliment *you*. I harass Sawyer. Is there anything else I can do for you, my queen?"

Ilse suppressed another smile, considering her tentative position. "I—I wish I could say. I just... I'm not sure I got this one. It feels wrong."

"Well," Rudiger said, "you and Tommy have done well together in the past. I'm sure you'll solve the case."

"Thanks... I sure hope so." Ilse paused for a moment. Then, frowning, she said, "Say—one last question. You said you looked at disability claims and lawsuits. Were there any accidents reported for *other* injuries at scrapyards? Maybe not loss of limb. But anything... *drastic*?"

"Drastic? Hmm. Well, someone climbed into a car crusher to retrieve a bag of weed and turned into goo."

Ilse winced. "I—I'm not sure that fits."

"Well... there's another scrapyard that had a fire... but it's closed down now. So probably not that either. What about—"

"Hang on," Ilse said suddenly. "Another scrapyard? You mean besides the ones we've found bodies in?"

"Yes, dear. But a defunct one. It's closed."

"No, I caught that the first time. Just... what about it? Why was it closed?"

"Umm—tralalala..." Rudiger sang a little ditty to fill the space as he searched once again for the appropriate information. "Ah—yes, voila. Here we go, my lovely. The scrapyard was closed down years ago after a fire. It's long been abandoned it seems. For about seven years."

"And the property is just sitting there?"

"No one ever did anything with it. It's just there... lingering... That's a funny word, isn't it? Lingering. Like lingonberry."

"Umm, yeah. Right. Thanks, Rudy. Mind texting me the address for that place?"

"Of course—It's... it's late there, isn't it?"

Ilse checked her phone and winced. They were rapidly approaching midnight. She still felt the exhaustion from a fitful previous night. Still felt the aches from their vehicle collision. But this needed to be done. Someone had to dig deeper. If they had the wrong suspect, that meant the real killer was still out there on the prowl.

On the hunt.

"Thanks Rudy. I'll be fine. Just send me the address. See ya!"

She hung up, pausing by the interrogation room door. She could hear Sawyer still pressing. Could hear a high-pitched voice responding rapidly to every accusation. Sawyer sounded like he was making progress... Maybe they had the right guy after all.

She lowered her hand from where she'd been reaching for the handle.

No... no sense in bothering him with something so silly.

Just a quick look. That was all. An old, abandoned scrapyard. What was there to find anyway? Mostly just a shot in the dark.

But the killer knew his junkyards. Had done his research. Undoubtedly, he would've found the same thing as Rudy.

What if he *had* found it. What if there was another monument there?

What if they were all completely off-base?

Ilse gritted her teeth.

She turned away from the interrogation room. Sawyer could finish the questioning. He'd been doing this sort of thing long before Ilse had ever joined up.

She just needed to swing by the scrapyard. Just to check. To assuage her curiosity.

Little Hilda Mueller was no longer so scared of the dark.

She clenched a fist, her teeth still set as she picked up the pace, rapidly marching down the hall and hastening towards the exit.

CHAPTER TWENTY SEVEN

The alarm continued to go as the survivor waited for the car salesman to emerge. After a few seconds, the locks clicked. The alarm was shut off.

He pressed against the smooth passenger door of the SUV, listening, waiting. The pungent odor of lighter fluid still filled his nose. He smirked at the sound of approaching footsteps. A pause, a faint exhale.

"Damn kids," a voice muttered. He heard a shoe scrape through the shards of glass followed by more dark muttering. A piece of the reflective material was sent skittering as the dealership owner kicked it away in disgust.

The survivor was patient. He always knew how to wait. He pressed his tongue against his lips, listening, waiting. He heard another long breath. The sound of fingers tapping against a keypad.

The shadow beneath the car, cast by the lights in the dealership, shifted.

And that's when the survivor moved. He preferred when they weren't looking. When he could sneak up behind them. Life had dealt him a bad... hand.

But when one got lemons, as the saying went...

He moved rapidly from behind the parked car, bringing his weapon out in the same motion from where it lodged in the leather seam inside his sleeve.

"Come on, come on..." the car salesman was muttering, holding his phone up as if looking for reception. "Cheap ass AT—"

He cut himself off mid-sentence, turning sharply at the sound of footfalls. The car salesman's eyes widened.

The survivor hit him, hard, across the side of the face. Something cracked. The salesman cried out. The survivor offered no mercy, though. He brought the weapon around a second time, clipping the man on the side of the forehead.

He fell like a sack of flour, hitting the ground with a grunt. The phone clattered off beneath the car. The alarm was silent. The dealership empty.

Another successful hunt.

"Good job," he muttered to himself. He nodded. "Thank you, thank you." He smirked, staring down at the bleeding salesman. Red liquid seeped through dark hair, spilling down the man's cheek and staining the ground.

He wondered how long it would take for anyone to realize the man was missing. "Tut, tut," he whispered. "All work and no play..."

And then, steadying himself with a breath, he reached for the key the salesman had used to shut off the alarm. At the same time, he grunted, using his arm to drag the man towards the SUV. One quick tug. A pause, a heavy breath. Another tug.

Things were harder for him than most. But hard had also made him tough. Hard was why he attacked from behind. Hard was why he couldn't let them be awake through the process. No, no. Even tying rope with one hand.

He felt a flash of phantom pain and rage. His muscles tensed; his neck tightened. He yanked again, again. More violently. Blood speckled the ground. He unlocked the back door of the SUV, which still stank of gasoline.

"Think you got away with it, don't you?" he whispered. "Think you're so clever. No—not clever. You're coming with me."

He finally managed to shove the dealer into the back of his own merchandise. Another machine. Sometimes, though, machines had to be managed in order to function. Machines had helped him on this purge, after all.

Just another little trip. A short stint.

He was going to take *this one* home with him. Like a stray puppy. Or cattle to be butchered.

He paused, leaning against the door with an elbow, breathing heavily. Hard to leave fingerprints when you only had five.

Then, shoving the man's legs unceremoniously after him into the back of the SUV, he clicked the keys, unlocked the front seat, and slid in. The lighter fluid stung his nostrils and he rolled down a window. He'd burn his clothes too, so he didn't mind sitting in some of the liquid.

He'd had far worse things stain his clothes in the past.

He put the car in gear and pulled out of the dealership, peering carefully through the windshield. No sirens. No onlookers.

People really didn't pay attention. Especially not to machines. A car like this was just a familiar thing to most folk nowadays.

He pushed the gas slowly, cautiously. The increasing speed caused his stomach to turn. “Not too fast,” he muttered to himself, irritated by the fear in his own voice. “Not too fast, please.” He sneered, “Alright, alright grandma.”

He slowed, moving five below the speed limit. He adjusted the rearview mirror, making sure his cargo was still unconscious.

Then, finally allowing himself a truly self-satisfied smirk, he maneuvered away from the dealership. No GPS for him. No phone. He knew this city by heart. He never would have trusted a device to tell him where to go.

No. He made his own path.

And all roads eventually led home.

***

Ilse picked up the speed in her borrowed car, wincing as she leaned in to study the GPS suctioned to her windshield. Ahead, a cop was sitting on the side of the road. She noticed it begin to roll forward. She cursed, reached out, flipping on her lights briefly. A flash of red and blue and the cop car went still, allowing her to pass.

She let out a long breath of air, hastening rapidly through the night, hurrying towards the address Rudiger had provided. When she'd left, their suspect still hadn't cracked. Sawyer was making headway though.

But she still couldn't shake the urge that they'd missed something. The one-armed killer... it made sense. How many scrapyard employees could be one-armed? She wasn't being silly; she was being cautious.

She moved faster now, veering around a slow-moving jalopy. One of the only other cars still on the roads this late at night. She glanced at her dash.

Past midnight. Night had come complete.

She shot a look at the GPS. Only ten minutes now. It wasn't like she expected to find anything.

Just a quick look. That was all. Covering their bases. She nodded, trying to convince herself it was all going to be just fine. They probably had the right killer. This probably was just a waste of time. She was doing it to be thorough, that was all.

And yet she couldn't shake the icy grip around her gut. The same sort of feeling she had so often felt when her father had returned home. When she'd heard the slamming door upstairs. The footsteps against the concrete steps.

Her stomach twisted again as the digital clock on her dash kept ticking.

***

He slammed the door behind him, letting out a long puff of air. The night had gotten chilly all of a sudden, and his breath fogged above him. He stared curiously at the rising mist.

Soon, smoke would follow.

He smirked, turning back to face the SUV he'd borrowed from the car lot. The scent of lighter fluid now clung to his clothing, simmered in his nose. But it was worth it. The point he was making was worth it. Man versus machine.

The dealership owner hadn't checked the vehicle he'd sold. A lemon with a perforated gas tank.

That little old lady hadn't stood a chance.

"Immolation," he said, stretching his lips and enjoying how it felt. "Imm... ol...ation." He chuckled to himself, standing within eyesight of his very own home, built in the side of the abandoned junkyard. The place had once burned down.

A fitting end given what he had planned. He reached into his pocket with his good hand and pulled out a lighter, holding it up to his face. He sparked the thing a couple of times and then stared at the little whisper of flame shuddering and shivering in front of his mouth.

Then, he looked directly at the SUV.

This was always the best part. He took a step towards the vehicle.

And he heard a faint groan. He stared, stiffening. Another, longer, pained groan. Then a hand flopped out the back window which he'd opened for the breeze against the pungency. Another groan. The door clicked, swung open like the lid to a coffin.

And a blood-soaked figure rolled out of the backseat, flopping onto the dusty ground like landed perch.

He stared. He must not have hit the man as hard as he'd thought. Or maybe the dealer just had a particularly tough nature.

He felt a flash of fear now, as the man's eyes turned towards him, fluttering. Another groan. Then a strangled, gasped word, "H-help me. P-please..."

The survivor felt a lance of absolute terror.

They weren't supposed to look at him. Weren't supposed to speak to him. He didn't do this face-to-face. No... No, no, no. Not when he was crafting... not while creating. Only before. Never after! Never!

Shit. Shit. He felt his teeth grind against one another. Felt a trickle of drool down the corner of his mouth. "No," he said out loud. "No, you can't be awake!"

"Please. Help me." The blood had caked the back of the man's neck and shirt. And yet he was pushing up off the ground. Pushing with *both* his hands.

And suddenly, to make matters far worse, a flash of lights illuminated off a scrap wall. He froze, turning sharply to look back down the hill. Another flash of lights. Then the sound of wheels against the road.

His heart leapt. Panic set in. Fear like he always felt. Fear like he lived with flooded him. The same fear he'd felt when that mechanic had neglected the safety check. When his hand had been lost.

A fear that went into the bones. A deep, blood-chilling terror.

"No, no," he murmured. "No!"

A car was moving up the hill. Someone was here. Someone was at *his* home. No one came here. Why? Why?

Another groan from behind him. The car wheels spinning before him.

Everything closing in. Too fast. Too much.

He wanted to scream. He took a hasty step towards the groaning dealer, his weapon appearing from the small leather holder inside his sleeve. But as he hefted his weapon, the car's headlights dipped lower. Soon, they'd illuminate him completely when the vehicle crested the hill.

Another jolt of panic. Of sheer terror. He turned on his heel and, with a squeak of fright, bolted, hurtling into the junkyard to hide. He knew this place like the back of his hand.

And he never got visitors.

So who the hell was trespassing?

CHAPTER TWENTY EIGHT

Dr. Ilse Beck frowned through her windshield, trying to make out the dark, looming shapes of the abandoned scrapyard in the dead of night.

Ilse stared over the crest of the hill, her heart in her throat. She could've sworn she had seen movement. But where was—

A sudden sound startled her.

What was that? She winced, bringing the car to a complete and jarring stop by slamming on the brakes. The tires rolled over something lumpy. She froze and tentatively pushed open the door, peering alongside her car, fearing the worst...

She let out a long sigh.

It was just an old garbage can lid. The rest of the can was upside down in a bed of charred junk.

Now with the door open, the chilly evening air gusted through the car. Her headlights illuminated the space, and highlighted an SUV parked across the clearing beneath piles of refuse.

As she pushed slowly out of the vehicle, inhaling the night air, she detected an odor of ash and grease. The place smelled and looked of neglect.

Shivers trembled down her back as she stood open and exposed in the dark. Her headlights illuminated the other car, but no one was inside it.

"Hello?" she called out softly. "Hello, is anyone there?"

No response. A faint whistle of the wind as it moved through rigid protrusions. Her phone buzzed and she nearly jumped out of her skin. She slapped a hand to her thigh, and pulled out the device, her fingers trembling.

A single text message. From Rudiger.

"Are you okay?"

She hesitated, then instead of answering, slipped the phone back into her pocket. She took a tentative step towards the SUV. Perhaps Rudiger was right. Perhaps she should call someone. Why was there a car here?

She began to reach for her phone a second time; then her gaze was caught by a lump.

A dark shadow stretched across the dusty ground.

Her heart hammered wildly. She swallowed back a shout.

A body. Caked in blood.

No sign of movement. No sign of the killer.

"Hello..." she said, more urgently.

No reply from the body.

She bolted forward, putting caution to the wind. She dropped to a knee by the form. The scent of blood was also accompanied by a faint, pungent odor.

The same stench was exuding from the open back door of the SUV. Blood left a trail along the dirt towards the car. The headlights from her own vehicle illuminated the horrible scene.

The figure at her feet suddenly groaned, rolling onto his back. Her heart jolted. The man stared up at her, his lips quavering. He gasped, trying to speak.

"Don't move," she said quickly. "I'm calling for help!"

The man on the ground was trying to speak. His eyes kept moving as if he were trying to indicate something. For a moment she paused, trying to decipher the motions. But he had lost too much blood already. He was delusional.

She pushed to her feet, raising the phone above her.

This sudden motion in search of reception saved her life.

Something swished past her shoulder, swiping through the air where her head had been seconds before.

A fast-moving shape.

A curse. Another swish.

This time she spotted the motion. She flung herself back, stumbling away.

She shouted as she tried to move for her weapon.

But the figure had come up from behind her.

A one-armed man was charging at her. A thin, frail, scrawny man. He looked like a skeleton in a sweater. A hood was thrown up over his face.

His lips were stretched, his cheeks gaunt. He screamed as he charged her. And this time, whatever he was holding connected across her chin.

Pain. She stumbled. The scent of ash, of char, of chemicals was now replaced by the stench of human body odor.

She tried to protect herself as he swung at her again.

She caught the blow on her arm, but this prevented her from reaching her weapon.

He seemed to realize she was armed, and redoubled his efforts, screaming now, "You're ruining everything! Go away! You can't do this!"

She didn't have time for conversation. She did everything she could just to stay alive. She tripped, falling over the trashcan lid and bouncing off her car. She hit the ground. The killer screamed, stomping at her. She managed to pull her gun. But he was still moving towards her. He had a panicked, terrified, deranged look in his eyes. But he was like a cornered beast. His terror and fear only made him more ferocious. He kept coming at her, howling, swiping. Screaming.

He kicked her gun. Pure luck. She didn't think he'd been aiming for it. He'd just been flailing.

But her weapon launched, landing in a pile of metal.

Desperately, she looked for it. But she didn't have time. He tried to smash her skull again. She scrambled back on her hands and knees, kicking up dust, scattering pieces, yelling incoherently back at him.

The two of them shouted at each other, like a couple of animals trying to exert auditory dominance.

He kept gabbing on, shouting about how unfair it was. And she was ruining things.

She tried to push to her feet. But this time he intentionally shoved his boot into her chest and sent her flying back. Her shoulder blade struck an old dishwasher. Pain lanced down her arm.

She cursed, trying to get to her feet but he quite literally had the upper hand.

He was moving on the terrain like a goat. As if he'd practiced for just such a moment like a dancer familiar with his stage.

Ilse, though, kept stumbling, falling. She couldn't keep her balance on the uneven terrain. She tried to scramble back towards the dirt road, but he kept cutting her off, forcing her further onto the pile of junk.

This was his home turf. Her heart hammered horribly. He struck her again. This time her forearm jolted.

She wasn't sure if something had broken, or if the snapping sound had come from his weapon. But the pain was immense.

In agony, she tried to defend another blow.

Sooner or later, he'd score a shot to her head. If she fell unconscious, there was no saying what he would do.

"Get off!" she shouted. Desperately she searched for her gun but there was no sign.

She scrambled on old, rusted springs, nails, pieces of jutting metal, rebar, and abandoned steel beams.

Everywhere she tried to move, something threatened to trip or gouge or cut. The scent of char was immense. The rust horrible. Thoughts of being impaled on some unseen spike or sliced by some unnoticed edge made it even more difficult for her to dodge the attacks.

And then suddenly, she heard a shout. Followed closely by the sound of gunfire.

The killer above her froze, turning sharply.

Ilse risked a glance as well

A man in a baseball cap, wearing flannel and jeans, was marching towards them, his gun pointed in the air. He hadn't risked a shot with Ilse so close.

For one wild moment, she stared in disbelief, unable to believe what she was seeing. *Sawyer?*

And then it struck her. Rudiger. The tech whiz had contacted Tom. She felt a sudden flood of gratitude. She wasn't sure what she was more grateful for. That Rudiger had cared enough to call for backup on her behalf, or that Tom had answered a call from the flamboyant techie.

Sawyer shouted something incoherent, his gun still raised. He sprinted forward. The killer yelled and moved for the only source of cover remaining.

Ilse's car. And she had left the keys in the ignition.

CHAPTER TWENTY NINE

Ilse shouted a warning, terror flooding her system. Sawyer's eyes widened as he noticed what the killer was doing. He began to move, rushing towards cover behind an old, red dumpster.

But the killer gunned the engine, flooring the pedal.

The vehicle roared to life. Headlights flashed across the junkyard as the car circled back down the trail. Sawyer raised his gun, shouting. Ilse glimpsed the killer duck out of sight in the front seat, sheltering from the bullets.

The windshield shattered as Sawyer released a shot. The killer drove straight at Tom.

"Watch out!" Ilse screamed. Frantically, she pushed to her feet, still desperately looking for her own weapon.

Sawyer wasn't about to let the killer escape, though. Again, the same way he had back on the highway, he put himself in danger in order to curtail the suspect's escape route. He shoved the red dumpster, groaning with exertion.

The killer tried to circle around it, to race down the hill. The wind whistled through the shattered windshield. Dirt spat from the car's tires. And then, it slammed into the edge of the red dumpster, sending it spinning.

The car veered off to the side from the collision, rolling up onto one of the junk piles. Both the tires burst, and the vehicle lost momentum.

At the same time, the spinning dumpster struck Sawyer across the leg. He had tried to surge to safety, but just a second too late.

Ilse abandoned her weapon, sprinting straight down the hill towards her partner. Behind her, she could still hear the victim gasping for air. The man was bleeding. They needed backup.

Sawyer was on the ground, groaning, clutching his leg. Broken?

He was still moving it but agonizingly slowly. His whole leg would be one bruise in the morning. If they managed to reach morning.

As Ilse rushed towards Sawyer, another figure made his move.

The killer climbed through the shattered windshield. The doors were jammed against the junk, another one twisted and bent from where it had struck the dumpster.

Cursing, bleeding from glass cuts across his face and a single arm, the killer clambered over the hood. His footsteps made soft thumping sounds against the metal. He jumped to the ground, growling. He reached down, picking up a length of rusty rebar. He lifted the metal bar, like a spear, and began charging towards Sawyer.

The agent looked up, eyes wide. He yelled, scrambling back, but not making it far. His teeth were set against the pain in his leg.

Ilse was still sprinting. Only twenty feet away. Fifteen. The killer began to swipe. The rebar struck the ground. Dust exploded. Sawyer barely avoided the attack. Another swipe. Sawyer just barely missed being decapitated.

And then Ilse reached them. The killer was so busy trying to kill Sawyer, he didn't notice the small woman hurtling out of the night and slamming into him from the side.

He howled like a scalded cat. The rebar went flying. The two of them hit the ground in a tangle of arms and legs. Dust in her mouth. Ash in her nose. Something jamming against her throat. A thumb. He was trying to crush her windpipe.

She bit at the hand. A yell. Still struggling, fighting, rolling one way, the other.

But she had two arms to grapple with. He only had one. A small, bony man. Wild, desperate eyes. He was muttering, speaking in an incessant stream. But it didn't seem like he wanted a reply from her. Almost as if he was talking to himself.

He tried to choke her.

She broke the grip. She shoved him off, finally gaining the upper hand.

He wasn't armed anymore.

Sawyer was still trying to struggle to his feet, and had managed to make it upright, but was leaning against the dumpster for support. Ilse had the killer on the ground beneath her.

"Stop moving!" she demanded. "Stop it, now! Tom, are you okay?"

"Fine. Don't let the bastard go!"

Ilse shook her head. She pointed back up the hill. "Another victim. Still alive. But bleeding. We need paramedics."

Sawyer bobbed his head, nodding quickly, breathing heavily. Suddenly, the man beneath Ilse tried to buck his hips. She maintained her balance. He tried to claw her face. But she was able to hold back the one hand.

He tried to twist one way, the next.

But it wasn't difficult to keep him down. He was exhausted, stinky, slicked with sweat. He was desperate.

But this time he wasn't sneaking up behind her.

In a way, his efforts were quite pathetic. She was stronger than him. He couldn't do anything. If she wanted to, she could've held him there with a single hand.

A weak, small man. A desperate man.

And yet she could see the hatred in his eyes. The sheer, simmering rage. She could feel the waves of vitriol coming from him, as spittle flecked her hands where she held him.

"Paramedics are coming!" Sawyer shouted. "They're flying a chopper in. No units are close enough to get here by road."

Ilse sighed, flashing a thumbs up.

Her own head was spinning. Exhaustion weighed heavy. She wanted to lay down. Wanted to go to sleep.

But just a little bit longer.

The man continued to fight, to push, and then suddenly he went still, limp.

It was the strangest thing, like watching a child throw a temper tantrum and then fall asleep.

One moment he was foaming at the mouth, cursing, spluttering, kicking, and shoving. The next, he went still. Motionless, and quiet. Tears appeared in his eyes as he glared up at her. Tears of anger.

"You're under arrest," Ilse said, "in case that wasn't clear."

He tried to spit at her, but she pushed his head off to the side, and kept him there.

It seemed odd that someone who had caused so much pain, so many deaths, was so weak. Small. Defenseless in a way. Without a weapon, or his machines, or his welding tools, he was just a helpless little man.

Sawyer hurried over to her now, helping her restrain the fellow and turn him on his back. The two of them cuffed one of his ankles to his hand, forcing him to lay in the dust.

They didn't have time to be nice about it, they needed to help the other victim.

Sawyer held a hand firmly against the killer's back. "Go!" he called, "Go, I've got him!"

Ilse nodded; she turned up the hill, and breathing heavily, broke into a jog. She rushed through the scrapyard at night, hastening towards the bleeding man at the top of the hill.

There was no rest for the weary.

Nor the wicked.

But this time, she had gotten here in time. This time, someone had survived. At least for the moment.

Where was that damn helicopter?

She reached the side of the bleeding victim and dropped to a knee. She began talking, trying to keep him conscious. "Help is on its way," she kept saying. For a head wound, moving the body would be a mistake. She just had to keep him there. She couldn't even wash the wound. Too risky. So all she could do was wait.

Sometimes, pain was the worst.

Other times, it was waiting. Not pain, but all the possible pains.

But she had no choice. She waited in the dark junkyard, ash on the air, dust in her mouth, a bleeding man at her knees.

She closed her eyes, murmuring softly to keep him awake. "It's going to be okay," she said. "It's going to be fine."

She remembered another time, in a dark basement, when her older siblings had crawled next to her after a particularly bad beating. They had whispered the same things to her. And they'd been telling the truth. For Ilse it would be okay. But for many of them, it had ended not much longer after.

Some people survived.

Others didn't.

It wasn't her job to question why. It was just her job to help those who lived.

CHAPTER THIRTY

Ilse sat on the bench outside the hospital, her foot tapping nervously against the concrete. She kept glancing towards the sliding doors as nurses and doctors and patients and visitors came in and out.

Where was he? What was taking so long?

A few seconds passed. She glanced at the clock on her phone.

A few more moments passed. And then Agent Sawyer appeared.

Tom was limping, using a cane to walk. He had a brace on his right leg, and a couple of bandages visible just past his neck. But otherwise, he seemed in good spirits.

"How are you doing, doc?" he said, as he approached her, moving through the sliding glass doors.

Ilse pushed to her feet and nodded. "Fine. You took your time."

He snorted. "Sorry my injuries don't heal on your schedule."

Ilse shook her head. "Do you want a ride or not?"

Tom grumbled, but it was good-natured, humorous. He allowed her to lead him back towards the waiting car.

Ilse smiled as they moved. Nearly forty-eight hours had passed since they had captured the junkyard killer—he'd confessed in the first few seconds of questioning. Ranting and raving about machines, about survivors. The would-be victim had survived, but the path to recovery would be slow. Still, forty-eight hours had been a long time. Sawyer's insistence that nothing was wrong with him after the first night had given away to an emergency call in the middle of the night about pain in his leg.

Ilse had spent the better part of the morning waiting outside the hospital for him to emerge. And now, she shot him a sidelong glance. "I'm guessing it's not nothing."

He grunted. "Good observation."

"What is it with men and pain? You guys can't handle it, but you pretend like you don't have it."

Sawyer snorted. "What's it with women and putting all men in one box?"

"If I could fit you all in a box I would," Ilse replied. "At least that way I could keep an eye on you and make sure you're okay. So really, what was the problem?"

Sawyer sighed, rubbing at his leg and reaching Ilse's parked car ahead of her. The boat. A beige Toyota Avalon with a wide turn radius. It had been her car for a few years now. She cherished it like most people did their pets.

She opened the door for Tom and allowed him to slip into the passenger seat.

"It's fine," Sawyer said. "There was a piece of bone floating around in my ankle. About the size of a quarter." He held up his fingers, forming a circle.

Ilse moved into the driver seat and slammed the door. "A floating chunk of bone? You were *walking* on that thing."

He shrugged. "Doctor says I should keep the cast on for a few months. We'll see. Last cast I had I cut off with a hacksaw."

Ilse grumbled, putting the vehicle in gear, and turning away from the parking spot. "Of course you did," she said. "A hacksaw. Why not. It makes perfect sense."

Sawyer grunted in affirmation.

Ilse tried not to roll her eyes too hard. No sense in spraining anything.

The two of them got comfortable as Ilse turned out of the hospital and merged onto the highway.

Sawyer's home was only a few minutes from here. Part of her wanted to take the long route. She wanted a chance to talk to her friend. She shot him a sidelong look as they drove. He looked contented enough, his fingers drumming against the curve of his walking stick. His one leg extended far in front of him, and he slid his chair back as far as it would go to give his lengthy frame ample room to stretch.

Ilse shifted uncomfortably in her seat, wondering just how much Sawyer was in the mood to tolerate. She didn't want to pry, but she was still troubled. That look in the killer's eyes. That deep, vengeful rage. She had caught it in Sawyer's gaze as well whenever he talked about his sister and the man who had killed her.

As far as she knew, Rebekah's killer was still in prison. He would be for life. But Sawyer needed help. Needed to open up, and yet she knew, like everyone else in her profession, she couldn't force someone to *want* help; they had to reach that conclusion on their own.

She shifted again, gripping the steering wheel as she guided them through the city, back towards Tom's apartment.

"How are you feeling?" she said slowly.

Ilse received a grunt in response.

She pressed on, "There's no easy way to say this, Tom, but I wanted to talk to you about something..."

"Your father's hearing?" Sawyer turned to look at her.

She winced uncomfortably. She would have to catch a flight tomorrow in order to arrive at the hearing on time. The flight was already booked, and she couldn't miss it. Already, she had rehearsed what she would say. Over and over, she had thought through how she would present her case when confronting that monster.

She still didn't know who was sending her the postcards. Didn't know if it was even related to her father's parole. But she'd decided to attend one issue at a time.

"Not about that," she said.

Sawyer grunted again. "Have your tickets lined up?"

"Yes. I do. Look, Tom, my itinerary is handled. I'll be there in time to reach the prison for the hearing."

Tom said, "Make sure to leave plenty of time for security. Those sorts of things can take longer than you think. Not just at the airport, but at the prison."

"Oh, well, yes... Did you used to work prison security?"

Sawyer shifted uncomfortably. "No. Just past experience." He frowned, going quiet again. And once more, Ilse was struck at how strangely he was acting. One moment asking her about her life, but the next closing down as if she had said something to offend him. Why was the prospect of working in a prison so offensive?

She never really could understand Tom. She liked him well enough. Perhaps that was why it bothered her so much—she didn't want him to get hurt.

She soldiered on. "Tom, I really think you could benefit from talking to someone."

The moment she said it, she winced. Sometimes, hearing out loud what she'd been thinking could give a new perspective. And now, having said it, she heard how presumptuous it sounded.

Sawyer didn't look offended. He just went quiet. "Not a big fan of talking."

"I mean about your sister," she said, wincing again but she pressed further. Now it would take courage to make the point.

Sawyer was staring out the window. "I know what you meant."

"I'm glad. Please, Tom. I'm only saying it because I care. I want to see what's best for you."

"Rebekah was best. And now she's gone." Sawyer shrugged one shoulder. He shook his head, still staring out the window. "Sometimes we don't have that choice, doc."

Ilse felt her heart hammer. She shifted again. "Tom, please. I can see it's eating at you. It distracted you on this case. You need to," she paused, trailing off. They were always trained that phrases like, *you should,* or *need to,* were best to be avoided in delicate situations. "If I were you," she said, reframing, "I would want to talk to someone about it."

He looked at her. "Have you?"

Two short, curt words. And yet they cut.

"It's my job."

"That's not what I asked. Have you talked to someone? About all that stuff that lingers up there." He pointed at her head. "I don't know most of it, doc. About your father. You don't mention this stuff. I know it's bad. Anyone can tell it's bad. Your ear—one has to wonder how that sort of thing happens."

She brushed her hair past her injured ear. She felt uncomfortable. Now it was Sawyer who was prying into her life. That wasn't why she had opened the topic.

He wasn't playing fair. But a small part of her realized that was exactly what he was doing. And now she was feeling what he had been.

She didn't like the sensation.

"Tom," she said, trying again, more insistently this time, "you have to believe me, I'm not trying to give you more problems."

He looked away again. "You've got your demons. I've got mine. You handle them your way. I'll handle them my way."

Ilse shifted uncomfortably. "What's your way?"

He looked at her. "What's yours?"

She drifted off in the silence, still driving.

This was going poorly. Sawyer hadn't opened up at all. And now she felt uncomfortable with her own position. It was true that she didn't fully open up about everything. A lot of her memories were still buried, lost. She didn't want to remember. It hurt too much. Besides, there was no healing from some of them. Only time would help. At least, so she told herself. And yet the idea of ever sitting down across from someone, and dumping her guts, revealing every little sordid detail, made her want to vomit. She had never even done that with Dr. Mitchell. Not with Sawyer. Not with anyone.

She wasn't married, so she didn't have that requirement of mutual honesty tugging at her conscience. She didn't date, so there were no uncomfortable questions while getting to know one another. Her relationships were with colleagues. Or clients.

And with her clients, she was the one who had the answers. She was in control. Just as she liked it.

She frowned as these thoughts cycled through her mind. She didn't like the way it painted her. But what if Sawyer was right? What if she was trying to hold him to a standard that she refused to meet in her own life?

Dammit.

Sawyer was still staring out the window, and Ilse drifted off into her own silence. They moved quickly through the streets. Ilse tried not to speed, but she wanted to get Tom home so she could return to her apartment to pack.

She wasn't sure what her way of dealing was. Maybe it was clients. The cases. Saving as many as she could.

She shook her head, and nearly missed their turn. Sawyer said, "This is it."

She slammed the brakes, quickly apologizing and hitting her blinker as she turned onto the side street that led towards Tom's apartment. She pulled along the curb and turned to face him. "I hope you feel better soon."

He was watching her again. He didn't look angry at her. If anything, he looked sad. He cleared his throat, one hand against the windowsill. "I don't know," he began, then trailed off. He paused, considering his words, then said, "I'm not sure what's gonna come after all of this."

"After what?" she said, thinking of the case. The most recent confession from the most recent killer.

He shrugged. "You know, if this is the last time we see each other in this way, I just want to let you know, it's been all right. You've done a good job."

Ilse stared at him. "Why would this be the last time we saw each other?"

He immediately balked, shaking his head. "I mean, you're heading off to Germany. You keep heading back. I don't know. I'm just saying," he said, irritated now, "you've been all right."

Ilse didn't want to let it go. She stared at her partner. He wasn't suicidal. He didn't have the markers. He was a man of action. What was he planning on doing?

A slow chill of dread trembled up her back. "Be smart, Tom."

He winked at her. "Always," he said. "Look, your flight tomorrow—hope it's a good one. Safe travels."

He stuck out a hand as if to shake. She stared at the hand. Was it a farewell? Why was he still acting this way? More than ever, she wished she had managed to get him to open up, to talk

But in the end, she just took his hand and shook it once. "Stay safe, Tom."

He chuckled. "You know what, doc, you're cute when you're worried."

She wrinkled her nose. "You sure know how to speak to the ladies."

But Sawyer wasn't smiling. He wasn't teasing like they so often did. He was just watching her, his eyes hooded, his voice low. He let out a shaking little breath. "You really are something," he said.

"Don't worry," she said. "The parole will just be a day. I'll be back by the weekend."

He flashed a thumbs up and a nod. And then he pushed open the door, waving as he left.

As he walked away, Ilse felt uncomfortable. Strange.

He thought she was *cute* when she was worried?

From someone like Rudiger, a comment like that might've just been harassment, or play. From Tom?

Cute. She wasn't sure she'd ever thought of herself as cute. Others said she was pretty, given that she didn't wear makeup or do her hair in the way that was expected.

But she also had never dated anyone. Not in more than thirty years. She had been convinced living alone, single, would be the only way to keep others safe.

She hadn't wanted to harm them.

Now all the thoughts she had about Sawyer came rushing back. But this time it felt like staring into a mirror.

Healing only happened with vulnerability. Only happened in community. She thought of what Dr. Mitchell had told her. How something lost didn't necessarily mean something couldn't keep growing. Some of the largest oaks in the forest lost branches when they were young.

She stared after Sawyer, brushing her hair behind her ear. Normally she tried to hide her face.

She smiled to herself.

Cute. It was nice to hear.

The smile flickered though, and the worry returned. Sawyer moved into his apartment, without looking back.

Agent Tom Sawyer was going to do something. She just didn't know what. Should she call someone? Who? Rawley?

She sighed, shaking her head.

Sawyer was a big boy. An agent. He could take care of himself.

Besides, she couldn't control other people's choices. She had a suitcase to pack. Her plane left bright and early tomorrow morning.

She put the car in gear, and pulled out of the parking lot, turning back onto the street to head home.

CHAPTER THIRTY ONE

Ilse stepped through the sliding doors of the airport, dragging her luggage behind her. She exhaled, preparing for the stressful few hours it took to navigate customs and security and to reach the plane. She always liked to give herself at least three hours before the flight took off.

Still, she could feel her nerves stretched thin.

She rolled her suitcase towards the baggage area, hoping that she had managed to stay under the weight limit.

It wasn't like she had to bring too much with her for a couple of days in Germany. Most of the weight in her luggage was from her old, desktop computer. Her speech was on it. Her research. Everything she had compiled to make a case against Gerald Mueller.

She frowned as she walked across the slick floor, trying to avoid colliding with any of the other air travelers moving hurriedly about.

As she hastened forward, lugging the heavy suitcase, she wondered if perhaps Tom was right. Maybe it was time for a laptop.

But she could be stubborn with such things.

Before she could reach the check baggage area, her phone began to ring.

She paused, fishing it from her pocket. She came to a halt next to a large, load-bearing rectangular white column. A *Welcome to Seattle* sign was placed far above, out of reach. Smiling faces in high gloss stared out from the poster.

She answered her phone. "Hello?"

"Oh, hi," said an unfamiliar voice.

Ilse paused, wrinkling her nose. "I'm sorry, who is this?"

A quickly cleared throat. "Er, sorry, maybe I shouldn't have called. Is this Dr. Beck?"

Ilse shifted. "It is. I'm afraid I don't have your number saved. Who is this?"

"You," the voice hesitated, and trailed off, but then summoned some courage and tried again, "you were once my therapist. About five years ago. You worked with me."

Ilse hesitated. "Oh, all right. Is everything all right?"

"Fine. Yes. Just, well, I actually work at a law office downtown. And, it's not a big deal, but I noticed you had pulled my file. It pings the system whenever employee records are requested—the practice has a transparency policy."

Ilse hesitated, and then it struck her. While she had been searching for potential candidates for the postcard taunter, she had requested additional information, using some of her agency credentials. It hadn't been strictly by the book to use the FBI to solve a personal case, but she hadn't thought much of it at the time. Now, she could feel her cheeks reddening. "Dear goodness. I'm so sorry," Ilse said hurriedly. "I was just doing some background work."

"Oh, okay. I wasn't sure what it was about. It just flagged on my computer. I have it set up. You know, after some of the things we talked about." She gave a little chuckle. "It doesn't bother me as much anymore. But we all have some habits. Fears that are hard to put to rest."

"Working at a law office," Ilse said. "You sure have come far."

"Thanks to you," the voice said with another laugh. "I'm glad—glad that it was nothing serious."

Ilse smiled, feeling a soft warmth. A client of hers was doing well. She sounded happy. She was employed.

"I'm afraid I don't know who this is," Ilse said quickly. "Not to be rude. I was going through a lot of employee records and client files."

"No problem. It's Denise. Denise Salinger. We worked back in that lake house office of yours. Remember?"

Now that she said it, Ilse did remember a Denise. The woman she remembered, though, had been extraordinarily shy. She had dropped out of school twice. She had never finished a college degree. To satiate her own curiosity, Ilse said, "Things really have turned around for you."

"Yes," Denise said, embarrassed. "I was a different person back then. A bit out of shape, very depressed. Scared all the time. You did a great job. I would say ninety percent of it was your input. I never did thank you. I guess part of me calling was to do just that. It wasn't that strange to see that Dr. Beck had requested a file on me." She chuckled again. "Hopefully nothing came up."

Ilse thought back, and then laughed as well. "I think I spotted a couple of traffic tickets."

"Oh dear. I thought I paid those."

Ilse grinned. Another flash of pride. A call like this made her day. Her week. Reminded her that sometimes, the effort, the energy, the emotional investment paid off. Ilse lived for moments like these.

"Anyway, I should probably go," Denise said.

Ilse felt a sudden sadness at this. Her heart twisted. She couldn't think of any reason to keep talking, though, but quickly said, "One moment. Sorry. So sorry. I don't mean to keep you. It's just, I was wondering what made the difference? You give me a lot of credit. That's kind. But you did it. You changed your life. What was it?"

Even as she said it, Ilse wasn't completely sure if she was asking for herself, or for her clients.

Denise laughed. "I can't take much credit. I guess it was just talking to someone. As silly as that sounds. Talking a lot. Telling the truth. That was one of the big things. You told me I couldn't lie to you. And I especially couldn't lie to myself. I don't know if you remember," then Denise's voice went soft. "And honestly, I'm very embarrassed about this part, but you wanted me to tell you what I really felt about, you know, what had happened to me."

Ilse still couldn't remember the exact case involving Denise. It had been nearly half a decade ago, but she said, "Facing the truth of your emotions, it's a powerful practice."

"Actually, I was worried that was maybe why you had looked me up."

Ilse frowned. "Excuse me?"

"Because of what I told you. Remember?"

Ilse cleared her throat hesitantly. "I can't say I do."

There was another laugh, this one sounding like a sigh of relief. "Oh thank goodness. I was worried maybe something had happened to him."

Ilse's nose wrinkled. Her confusion only continued. "Happened to who?"

"The man who kidnapped me. I'm sorry, this is heavy. I'm really relieved that wasn't why you were looking me up. It was eating at me. I know I'm supposed to deal with anxiety without calling people out of the blue," another nervous little laugh. "But I was scared, honestly. I didn't want any of that to come up and affect my job. Five years of school, it's been hard. But fulfilling."

Ilse was still frowning. "You said something about the man who hurt you?"

"You don't remember. Well, at least that's okay. I don't feel like it at all anymore. At least not really. I don't think about it much."

"I'm afraid I don't understand."

The woman's voice dropped, to nearly a whisper, and there was a note of shame to her tone. "I never would've done it. I don't want to now. I was worried maybe something had happened and you thought I'd actually gone through with what I'd daydreamed about for years."

Vaguely, Ilse was beginning to remember. "Oh," she said, "*that*. I had completely forgotten about that. No, nothing to do with him. Forget about him. You don't have to spend another minute thinking about that guy. He's in prison now."

Denise gave another cheerful chuckle. "All right, well I've actually got to get back to work. It's silly, but I'm relieved to find that it was just some clerical work. Have a great day, Dr. Beck." She paused, then quickly added, "You saved my life. Thank you."

Ilse felt tears in her eyes, she blinked them back and cleared her throat as well. "Thank you for saying that. Really, thank you." They bid their farewells and hung up.

Ilse stood in the airport, luggage at her feet, staring towards the baggage check-in area. A quick flight, a booked hotel, and then bright and early the next morning her father's parole.

And yet something else was bothering her. Something niggling at her mind.

Something Denise had said. Or had helped Ilse remember. She had been scared that Ilse was looking her up because of a crime.

And Ilse remembered now. Denise had been trembling when she'd said it back in that lake office. Tears in her eyes. She had spoken as if she were revealing her darkest secret.

Ilse could practically see it now, could practically hear the swish of the leaves above the glass roof, the quiet lapping of the water against the shore. And then the words.

"I wanted to kill him. All I thought about for years is killing him. In horrible, horrible ways. It's all I could really think about before meeting you. I don't know what to do with that. The thoughts won't leave me alone. It's the only thing that will make me forget... why is it fair that he's allowed to live?"

Ilse opened her eyes, frowning.

By the sound of things, Denise had gotten better. Had moved on from the violent thoughts. It wasn't as if Ilse blamed her. She would never do that. But she was glad to hear the woman had put those ideas behind her. Through honesty. Through talking with someone about her pain.

Ilse felt another flash of gratitude but also a deep, unsettling sense of horror.

Sawyer had been acting strangely. For weeks. He kept bringing up his sister's killer. Rebekah was on his mind. The only thing on his mind.

Sawyer was planning something. She thought back to his strange farewell when she had dropped him off at his apartment.

She thought of the way he had examined the barbed wire outside the junkyard. How he had asked one of the employees about it. How he had gotten chummy with one of the gate guards, discussing entry points with him. Also, how he'd said goodbye... Like it would be the last time. He wasn't just going to act. But was going to act *now.* Why else would he have acted like he was on death row? She thought of Sawyer's temperament. A man designed for action. A man built on doing things, rather than waiting for them to be done.

Her heart pounded. Horror welled within her.

Sawyer wasn't going to hurt himself. Not intentionally.

He was going to hurt the man who had killed his sister.

Ilse was certain of it. Her bag toppled where she accidentally let go of the handle. The plastic grip tapped against the ground. A couple of passengers glanced in her direction, and she hurriedly ducked, picking the suitcase up.

A woman at the baggage counter was waving her over. But Ilse was rooted to the spot. Sawyer was going to do something that would ruin his life forever.

Dammit. But if she missed this plane, she was going to miss her father's parole. There were no other flights to Germany for the day. She wouldn't be able to make it in time.

She gripped the plastic handle on her luggage tighter.

Hastily, she dialed Sawyer's number.

No answer. She tried again.

No answer. For a moment, she wondered if she ought to contact Rudiger or Rawley. But that would be a surefire way to get Sawyer fired or arrested. No, she couldn't bring coworkers into this.

She cursed, trying to call Sawyer again. He wasn't answering. It was early in the morning, but he was an early riser. There was no reason he wouldn't be answering.

The baggage claim lady was still gesturing. But Ilse turned away, moving quickly. Her luggage trundled behind her as she marched back towards the sliding glass doors.

The flight would be missed. She wouldn't make it in time for her father's parole.

But Sawyer was going to kill his sister's murderer. She wasn't sure how, or how long he'd been planning it, but she knew he was going to try.

She broke into a jog, racing through the doors and hastening to the curb to flag down a taxi.

CHAPTER THIRTY TWO

Agent Tom Sawyer stared through the windshield at the large gray structure. His eyes traced the barbed wire, moved to the guard house, then landed on the brown, steel entrance.

Straight through, past the guard, fake ID, and then take it from there.

He rehearsed the moves in his head. Tom glanced to the blueprints on the seat next to him. He had pulled some strings to get these. The architect friend would be shielded from any fallout, but Sawyer was realizing the chances of getting out undetected were quickly diminishing.

He simply couldn't find a way to kill the monster and escape.

Still, he had made up his mind. It would cost him a lot.

He knew that much. His job certainly. His freedom definitely. Most of his friendships undoubtedly. The few remaining family connections he still had.

An exchange?

He felt a little shiver of relief. He would no longer have to live knowing the man who killed Rebekah was still breathing. Sometimes it was all he could think about; sometimes, when he tried to go to sleep, or close his eyes, all he could see was her body. All he could hear was that man taunting him.

He had targeted Rebekah to get at Sawyer. He had thought he had the last laugh.

But he hadn't accounted for agent Tom Sawyer's sheer will. Some thought of him as stubborn. Un-bendable. Rigid. But he just thought of himself as a man of determination.

He knew what he wanted. Now he just had to go and get it.

Sawyer pushed out of the car, trying not to notice the way his fingers were trembling.

He wouldn't be able to slip a weapon in there undetected. They didn't allow guns past the checkpoint outside maximum-security.

But it didn't matter. He didn't need a gun to kill a man.

Even as he thought it, he gave a little shudder. A voice, one that sounded all too like Dr. Beck, whispered in his ear.

This isn't you. It's your pain. You don't have to do this.

He snorted in derision, slamming the car door, locking it, and then moving purposefully towards the gates.

This *was* him. It was all he had been for years.

His stomach ached; his mind screamed. All he could think about, nights at a time, was this killer. The taunting. The torture. The things he had done to little Rebekah. She had been so kind.

Sawyer could feel tears coming. He didn't cry, not really. But like always, he suppressed the emotions. He inhaled deeply, held the breath, willing the feelings to go away.

And again, he was calm. Rigid. Unyielding.

He picked up the pace, moving rapidly towards the prison doors. The yards were clear. No one was on break yet. He glanced at his watch. In exactly twenty-five minutes, they would break. After lunch, the prisoners who were well-behaved would be given yard time.

Which meant the monster, his monster, would be left back in solitary.

He checked his pocket, making sure for the hundredth time he had the fake ID he had purchased.

His credentials would check out.

Rudiger would be the one logging the information on a computer.

Sawyer felt a surge of guilt at dragging the techie into it. But if anyone knew how to cover their tracks, it would be the flamboyant whiz. Besides, Rudiger didn't have a clue what Sawyer was doing. It hadn't felt good lying to the man. Telling him it was for a case. To try and get to someone that Rawley was holding behind bars. He had lied. Rudiger had believed him. He had never lied to his friend before.

Friends were not something he could allow himself to think about.

He reached the brown metal doors. Inside, he spotted men with guns behind bulletproof glass. He spotted an administration desk. He spotted metal detectors and the security checkpoint. Further on, more doors, more glass. More soldiers.

Because that's what they were. Soldiers. And he was here for war.

He reached out, pushing open the brown door, and stepping through. As it slowly closed, he blinked in surprise at just how thick the partition was.

One couldn't drive a truck through that thing.

He'd thought of that too. He'd thought of everything. One couldn't dig, because of twenty feet of concrete beneath the surface. The place was protected. The only way in was through the front doors.

Already, multiple cameras had caught him.

He'd thought about hiding his face. But there were cameras at chest height, cameras in the floor looking up. Cameras in the ceiling. If he tried to disguise his face, it would've only looked suspicious.

The fake ID was just to get him through since his own name would be flagged in relation to this prisoner.

Sawyer hadn't told Rudiger the true target. He'd given a fake story about a prisoner in a cell next to his real prey.

The fewer people that knew, the better.

The door swished shut behind him as he faced a metal detector and two security guards.

He stared, swallowed. He could still picture Ilse in his mind. The way he had bid her farewell. She had that look. The look she often carried. Like she had known what he was up to.

"Sir?" said a gruff voice. "You have an appointment?"

Sawyer nodded once, tipping his blue hat, and for the first time in years, he was wearing a suit, with a tie.

He removed his hat to reveal combed, Sandy hair.

He raised a clipboard, with his identification. "I'm expected," he said.

One of the guards waved him forward, gesturing towards the conveyor belt and an X-ray machine.

Sawyer approached, his hands no longer trembling. His stomach didn't hurt so much. He was a man of action. When he moved, his emotions went on sabbatical.

Now, all he had to do was see it through.

***

Ilse cursed, slapping the dashboard in a gesture of urgency, her eyes fixed on the road. “Can't we go faster?” she demanded, trying to keep her emotions under control.

The taxi driver looked at her, then returned his gaze lazily to the road. With one, outstretched finger, he tapped a worn sign taped to the ceiling.

We observe all speed limits. Safe travels!

The smiley face was a bit much, in Ilse's opinion. She continued drumming against the dash, feeling her heart in her throat. She glanced at the GPS.

Nearly half an hour away.

"Are you sure you have the right location?" she demanded.

The driver said, "Lady, we're going exactly where you told me."

Ilse checked her phone again. She'd gotten the address for the prison from one of the techs back at the office. Rudiger, strangely, hadn't taken her call. Was he in on it?

Shit. Sawyer was going to not only burn bridges, but also friends. He was going to get himself killed or arrested.

Thirty minutes... too long. Far too long.

Ilse shot the driver a glance. "Please," she said quickly. "Just a *bit* faster."

He began to reach up to tap the sign again, contentedly sitting in the right lane behind what must have been an old granny in a century old car. It moved at the speed of a carriage.

Ilse could feel her frustration mounting. She tried calling Sawyer again.

Still no answer.

Desperate times called for desperate moves... She winced, but then forced herself to focus. Tom needed her. They were going too slow. He wasn't answering his phone. Who knew if she was already too late?

"FBI," she said suddenly, ripping her ID from her pocket and shoving it in the driver's face. "Either pick up the damn speed or *I* will." She felt a flash of guilt and added, "Please."

As she lowered her credentials, the driver looked like he'd been slapped. Immediately, they veered around the slow-moving granny car and began hastening through traffic. Better... Much better. Ilse glanced at the GPS.

Twenty-nine minutes. A minute saved so far. "Faster," she murmured. "We need to go faster! But not too fast!" she added quickly with a horrible realization.

The last thing they needed was to be pulled over by a traffic cop. What would she possibly be able to do in that situation?

Umm. Sorry officer, just off to stop an FBI agent from beating a prisoner to death.

No... No, the fewer people involved the better. She could only hope it wasn't too late. By the silence of her phone, by the fact Rawley wasn't screaming in her ear, she supposed nothing had happened. *Yet.*

But she could feel time passing quickly by.

Another glance at the GPS.

Twenty-eight minutes.

"Come on... Come *on!*"

***

Sawyer dipped his head in gratitude as he accepted his wallet back from the guard. The man held up two of the plastic visas and the car keys. “We'll keep these for you when you return,” he said.

Sawyer nodded quickly, flashing a thumbs up. The guard at the door gestured towards a man sitting behind a bulletproof glass rectangular space. “He'll hook you up with a babysitter. Keep it tight.”

Sawyer nodded, returning his blue cap and moving towards the man behind the enclosure.

A door suddenly buzzed off to his right. Sawyer frowned. That didn't match the blueprints. He was supposed to be going left. He shot a look back towards the guards by the door.

Neither of them were looking in his direction now.

Sawyer let out a shaky exhalation. Suddenly, a figure emerged on his right. Another guard, this one armed with a baton and a walkie-talkie. The man moved past Sawyer to the *left* side of the enclosure, pointing towards the sealed door. “You with me, Rudy?”

Sawyer nodded once. He tried not to roll his eyes. Rudiger's sense of humor had even crept into the fake government IDs he'd provided. Oh well—they would get him in. That's all he needed.

The man behind the enclosure hit a button. The second door unlocked, rattling as the bars slid along a groove, giving Sawyer access to a hall.

The guard who'd joined him as an escort said, “Few quick rules—you're here to interrogate a prisoner. That's your business. I'm here to keep everyone safe and in place. That's my business. Got me? I'll let you ask questions. You let me do my job.”

Sawyer swallowed but nodded once. “Sounds good.”

“Man of few words. I like it. Let's go—this way. Prisoner 1083, right?”

Sawyer hesitated, swallowing. This was the rough part. He knew he couldn't have given Rudiger the proper prisoner number. Not without raising red flags and getting the techie to intervene.

“Prisoner 1093,” Sawyer countered quickly, frowning and trying to look as irritated as possible.

Irritated people often got their way. People preferred keeping them from blowing their top.

The guard, though, a veteran of dealing with manipulative behavior, didn't even seem to notice Sawyer's tone. He glanced at his file again, shaking his head. "I've got 1083," he said.

Sawyer shook his head and gestured over his shoulder. "I left my phone in the car. But we can call the boss, if you want. He set it up with the warden."

At the mention of the warden, the babysitter hesitated, gnawing on his lower lip. A gamble, but one Sawyer suspected would work.

He'd already been cleared. Already had access. Already had the proper information. What was a stupid number anyway? Interviewing a prisoner in one cell or the one in the cell next to him? All the same really...

At least, he was hoping an overworked staff at a maximum-security would see it that way. Their job was keeping the bad guys in. They also liked keeping FBI out. The sooner they got this over with, the better.

What did they care *which* prisoner in a ten foot space Sawyer had to speak with?

"The warden," Sawyer said again, "was hoping this would be a quick process. There's a girl in trouble." He flinched as he said the lie. Dishonesty did *not* come naturally to Tom. But in for a penny, in for a pound. "This bastard might know where she's being kept. Already been missing thirty-eight hours. You know how that goes..."

The guard let out a frustrated sigh, glancing towards the man behind the bulletproof glass. This other fellow just shrugged. The escort sighed, then said, "Fine. 1093. Same cellblock anyway. It always gives me the creeps how these guys still have their fingers in pies outside the prisons." The escort snorted as the metal door to the hall began to slide shut behind him again. "We think we're keeping people safe, you know..." he shook his head. "Really we're just keeping these bastards safe."

"Hang the lot of 'em," Sawyer muttered dispassionately.

The guard nodded in agreement, picking up the pace and launching into another stream of complaints. In a place like this, Sawyer imagined half the fun was the time to complain.

He didn't mind. He wasn't even listening.

Mostly, he was rehearsing the next step.

***

"This is it!" Ilse shouted. "There—there—no get me closer! Please. Closer!"

The taxi driver slammed on the brakes, perhaps a bit harder than was strictly necessary. He reached across to open the door for her, eager to be rid of her.

The feeling was mutual. They'd wasted so much time. Sawyer still wasn't answering his phone. She didn't recognize his car in the parking lot. But he wouldn't use his own car anyway.

She paid as quickly as she could and then broke into a dead sprint, without even bothering to shut the door, racing towards the prison. A large, gray structure. Tall, barbed wire. Bleak, brown metal doors.

Her feet pounded the pavement, but she slowed as she spotted men with rifles in guard houses. Cameras around her.

She exhaled in frantic huffs, brushing her hair behind her ear.

Now, she needed to make sure she didn't draw unwanted attention. Getting in, reaching Tom was one thing. What if he wasn't even here? What if she was going crazy?

But no, she had seen that look in his eyes. She had heard what Denise had told her.

She knew what was happening. If he wasn't here now, he would be soon. He had bid her farewell. Said his goodbyes. Tom had come into this knowing he wouldn't be getting out.

Was he even here?

She hurried towards the doors. They clicked, unlocking as she pushed in. Her identification held in front of her like some sort of shield, opened another set of doors.

She was confronted, though, by two guards standing by a metal detector. Other guards stood behind the bulletproof glass case.

She breathed heavily, trying to look professional. She wished she'd been wearing a suit rather than a sweater. But now wasn't the time to be concerned with such things.

"Hello," she said quickly. "Is Agent Tom Sawyer here?"

The guards by the metal detectors frowned. One leaned in, looking at her badge.

"What's it with feds today?" the guy muttered.

Ilse perked up. "The other guy," she said quickly, "the skinny tall one, did he just arrive?"

The guy behind the metal detector glanced at her ID again, at her sweater, and began reaching for his walkie-talkie. His partner, though, said, "Just got here a few minutes ago. You running late on your partner or something?"

Ilse stomach twisted. "Yeah, just a bit late. We said we would meet up here."

But now the guard was shaking his head. "I'm sorry, but if the warden doesn't approve it, you're not coming in here. We only have one slot for an escort. No other guards waiting by."

Ilse pressed her teeth tightly together. She didn't have time to make some calls.

She tried to keep her voice calm. "Did Agent Sawyer say how long he was going to be?"

"Agent who?" the guard said wrinkling his nose.

Ilse winced, realizing her mistake. "Sorry, Sawyer was the cover name he was using for our most recent case."

The guard relaxed. The one reaching for his walkie-talkie had his hand pressed against one of the buttons, but so far hadn't called anyone.

Ilse supposed that having FBI agents in their prison wasn't such an unusual event.

"Agent Rudy should be back after his interview," the guard by the door said with a shrug. "You can wait over there; take a seat. But you're not allowed any further. I'm going to have to ask you to step through the metal detector. Seeing as you're not pre-screened, we also have to frisk you. No weapons," he added.

Ilse nodded quickly, compliantly. She didn't have time to bicker. Sawyer was in here. Somewhere in the prison. He'd provided a fake name. Shit. She was running out of time.

She quickly unloaded her pockets, moving fast. And then, heart in her throat, wondering how on earth she was going to get Tom out of this, she stepped towards the metal detector and the two guards.

CHAPTER THIRTY THREE

Sawyer could feel his pulse quickening, his throat tight. He stared through the metal bars towards the hallway where only the worst of the worst were kept. Not even here were they allowed the privilege of vision. Lights were dimmed. The doors to their cells were giant blocks of steel. Only a slit in the base for food.

No sounds came from the cells. No movement. Nothing suggesting that monsters lurked in the dark. This time on top of the bed rather than under. Though in their cases, their beds consisted of little more than a springless mattress stuffed with non-choking material.

He felt his escort brush past him. "Forum says you wouldn't need a room." The guard gestured through the bars, sliding a set of keys in the locks then opening the door.

Now, nothing prevented Tom from stepping into the maximum-security solitary confinement wing. But he hesitated, one foot against the clearly painted red line. Words were written along the paint, but he couldn't read them. Couldn't focus.

He felt dizzy now, and reached out, bracing a hand against the wall.

Now came the hard part.

The guard had the keys. The escort stood to the side, bored, picking at his nose. He wasn't paying attention. This was the portion of the plan Sawyer had most dreaded. He knew how to put someone unconscious without harming them. He had no intention of hurting an innocent.

The guard didn't seem to detect any threats.

The plan had been to speak with the prisoner through the food flap. The slit halfway up the door also served to handcuff the inmates. They would turn, place their hands on the metal shelf, through the flap, and wait.

Now, it was to serve as Sawyer's interview platform.

But he wasn't here to talk through a metal flap.

No.

What he needed was *inside* that cage. He let out a faint little puff of air. His eyes darted up towards the camera blinking above the door.

He was being watched. He'd known this wouldn't be easy. Had known there wasn't a way out. He'd purchased a one-way ticket.

His fingers were trembling against his thigh. He shot another look at the guard, towards the keys back on his belt. Towards the walkie-talkie on his shoulder.

"You good, man?" the escort said suddenly. "Need me to wake the princess or something?"

Sawyer glanced towards the metal door, marked clearly with 1093. "I—no," he said. "That's fine. Thanks. I've got it."

He made as if to move across the red line. The escort glanced at his finger, seeing if he'd found anything while rummaging around his nostril.

Now. Now. Do it now! His subconscious screamed.

Sawyer took a tentative step towards the man, one hand bunched at the side. A quick punch, then a choke. He'd be out in no time. Sawyer let out a shaky breath... Now that he was faced with what he had to do, he wasn't sure he could go through with this part.

The guard hadn't done anything to him. Wasn't a bad guy. Hadn't had anything to do with Rebekah's death...

Sawyer could feel his frustration threatening to overflow. He just needed the guy to leave. Was that too much to ask? He unclenched his fist, thinking desperately now. Nonchalantly, he said, "Mind opening the cell?"

The guard look at him sharply as if he'd asked to strip naked. "What?" the guard said.

"The cell," Sawyer waved. "Open it. It's fine—I have the warden's permission."

The guard just stared, his eyes suddenly narrowing.

Even to Sawyer's ears, the lie sounded hollow. He could feel his heart rattling around in his chest a million miles a minute. He pressed his teeth together tightly, feeling a surge of anxiety. The guard's fingers were slowly inching towards his walkie-talkie. "You know protocol," the guard said slowly. "Right?"

Sawyer snorted, waving a hand. "Of course—of course. Just checking is all. It's fine. No, really—look I just need to speak with him. To make sure I'm talking with the right guy. You know how it is."

He tried to sound nonchalant, carefree. Dismissive even. But his throat was too tight. His heart pounding too much. He sounded scared. The guard was picking up on it now. The man stared at Sawyer with a deeply suspicious look in his eyes.

Sawyer should've just punched him from behind when he'd had the chance. But it would've felt... *wrong.* He needed to kill the monster in

1093. But he wasn't here to hurt some innocent trying to pay the family bills.

A new plan, then. The guard was spooked. Sawyer had used up most of his good will. Sooner or later, the guard was going to call someone that would check Sawyer's story.

No... no more stalling. No more wasted time. He'd snatch the keys, lock the door in front of him then open the prisoner's door. Yes. That was it. The only chance he had. It didn't matter if the guard saw all of it. Just so long as Sawyer had the keys.

That way, no one would get hurt who didn't need to.

Tom's hands tensed, he stared at the keys on the guard's belt. He tensed and then he lunged.

The walkie-talkie crackled. The guard moved to answer.

Sawyer missed, stubbing a finger against the wall. The guard hadn't even noticed. Sawyer was about to try again when he heard the voice echo over the speaker. "We have a request for Agent Rudy in the visitor's room. I repeat, a request for Agent Rudy in the visitor's room. It's urgent."

The guard glanced up, nodding and flashing a thumbs up towards a camera above them. The red light was still blinking. They were being watched. The guard had now removed his keys and was holding them.

Sawyer stared, his eyes bugging. Again, he nearly lunged for the keys, but the guard was holding them tight as he brought the cell block door swinging shut with a *clang*. He then began to lock it. "Well, well, you are quite popular aren't you, Rudy?" he said.

Sawyer blinked, taking a moment to recognize his own fake name.

"Wh—what? Someone wants to speak with me?"

The guard nodded. "That was the warden," he said. "Gotta do what he says."

"No—hang on. Wait! No—I need to speak with the prisoner!" Sawyer protested loudly, pointed a finger through the bars.

But the guard just shook his head. "Sorry man. Warden's orders are warden's orders. If he says someone's waiting in the visitor's room, then someone's waiting. You'll have plenty of time to talk to that scumbag later. It's not like he's going anywhere."

The guard chuckled and began walking away. Once more, his back was to Tom.

Sawyer clenched a fist. He knew this might be his only chance. Who was waiting to speak with him? Rawley? The warden? Had someone figured out who he was?

Shit... If he ended up in prison for *failing* to kill the monster, then he really would be giving that bastard the last laugh.

He inched up behind the guard who was whistling now, strolling down the hall, spinning the keys in a loop around one finger.

But again, as Sawyer stared at the back of the man's head, he simply couldn't bring himself to do it. How could he? He'd never intentionally hurt an innocent person before. Punching a bad guy was one thing. Punching a prison guard from behind?

The thought alone gave Tom anxiety.

He let out a long, shaking sigh. Then, reluctantly, fell into step behind the whistling guard.

Maybe it was just something clerical. Yes... that would be it. Maybe just a quick visit with the warden, answer some questions, and he'd be given another shot soon enough.

Sawyer inhaled shakily, exhaled as if panting. He wanted to turn and charge through the metal bars like some raging bull. But reality wouldn't allow him.

So instead, like a chastised school child going to see the principal, he walked gloomily after his escort, back down the corridor.

***

Ilse shifted uncomfortably in her seat in the visitor's room. The space was empty. They were off hours. This was the only compromise the guards had allowed. The tall tale she'd spun to get a phone call with the warden would've put her to shame on normal occasions. Ilse did not think of herself as a liar.

But now, having concocted some bullshit story about protecting the governor's missing daughter with the FBI, she was sitting in a visitor's room, waiting for her partner to arrive.

She could only hope the message had reached Tom before it was too late. Now, she was certain, if things had escalated before she'd arrived, she'd also be found culpable for whatever Sawyer had in mind.

The thought of ending up like her father, behind bars—whose parole she was now going to miss—made her stomach churn in anxiety.

She didn't have the constitution for prison. No... no she couldn't. Still, Sawyer had needed her. This was the best she could do for a friend.

Her foot tapped a tattoo against the greasy, tiled ground as she waited uncomfortably in the dingy, poorly illuminated space. The tables had no screws, no edges. The chair legs were padded in foam.

Such a strange, awful place.

She shifted again, shivering as she did, her unease swallowing any line of thought that didn't involve Sawyer and his immediate future.

Even thoughts of her father's parole, of the postcard-sender—all of it faded into the background.

Suddenly, a door buzzed. She jolted in her seat, whirling around to watch as a lanky figure was ushered into the room, prompted by a jail guard in a cream uniform. The guard was shooting strange glances at Tom Sawyer but didn't say anything as Sawyer moved from the hall.

"Five minutes," the guard said behind them. "Warden wants the space cleared when the inmates move to break."

Sawyer didn't reply. His eyes were now settling on where she sat.

Ilse just watched him. Tom didn't move, as if he'd been frozen in the doorway. He let out a shaking little breath and then approached the table. He moved as he always did, with confident, rolling strides.

But Ilse noticed his right hand trembling against his thigh.

He looked different now, wearing a suit and tie. Even his hair, beneath an ever-present cap, was slicked back. He'd pulled out all the stops.

She had to hand it to him. Tom was a man of will.

"Hey Rudy," she said slowly as he approached. The fake name tasted sour on her lips, but they were still in a precarious situation. The guard behind them was watching. Cameras around them were watching.

Sawyer didn't sit. He paced by the plastic table, as he so often did back in the interrogation room. He couldn't quite look her in the eye, it seemed. His fingers drummed against his leg as he stalked back and forth.

"What are you doing here?" he said in barely a whisper.

Ilse wasn't sure if Sawyer had already fulfilled his mission. Wasn't sure if things were too late. But she also knew that whatever she said could one day be used in a courtroom. So, cautiously, she murmured, "Seeing how you're doing. I hear you went to speak with a prisoner."

Sawyer's fingers continued their incessant tapping. "Doc, you don't know what you're getting into. You shouldn't be here..."

Ilse shot a look at the guard who was still watching them curiously. "Is there any reason we can't leave?" she said. Innocuous words but weighed with meaning. *Did you kill someone yet?*

Sawyer stared at her, then snorted. He went still, no longer pacing, and instead crossed his arms in a self-soothing gesture. "Damn, Ilse, I... no. Not yet. But I'm not leaving until I get what I'm here for."

Ilse crossed her arms now too.

Sawyer thought he was the only one who could be stubborn. Perhaps he was right. But she could endure with the best of them.

"Alright then," she said simply. "I'll wait until you're done."

His brow flickered. "I don't think you're hearing me, Ilse. You need to *leave* now."

"Too late for that. I'm here. I'm talking to you." She waved a finger around the room, indicating cameras. "If you go down," she murmured, "It's a two-person wreck."

Sawyer tensed now at this. His fingers went still against his leg. His breath came in rapid puffs, and she read the look of frustration across his features.

"Dammit, Ilse!" he snapped. "You shouldn't have come! You're tying my hands here..."

Ilse kept her cool. Kept calm. "I'm sorry, Tom. Sorry for interrupting. But this isn't the way. You know it isn't. You just don't know what else to do about it. I can help."

Sawyer was stalking again, like a big cat in a cage. His shoulders rolled as he moved.

"Three minutes!" The guard called from the doorway.

Sawyer didn't even seem to hear. He said, "You don't get it. You can't. This is the only way. Otherwise, he wins."

"Tom, you won. That's why he's here. Look around you. This is a hell hole. No one wants to be here. His choices brought him here. He beat himself. It's not about winning against someone else. It's about winning against yourself. He's tricked you into thinking you two are in competition with each other. You're not. The only person you need to worry about is you, Sawyer. Of course, that guy wants you to compete. He already lost his own race. He's here. He did those things. You... you're still in control of your own life."

She pointed at him now, the finger firm, unyielding just like his temperament. "This can't happen."

Sawyer let out another shuddering breath. She could see him warring with himself. She knew that with her here he wouldn't do anything rash. Not now. Not anything that would endanger her... At least, she didn't *think* he would.

Sawyer wasn't the sort to hurt an innocent to get his own way.

But on the other hand, she could see the pain in his eyes ripping him apart. The anger, the rage that had built up over the course of years. He'd never allowed it out. Never allowed anyone else to come near.

That was the angle. Ilse knew it. She'd experienced it many times before with clients. When hitting an obstacle, an emotional wall that resulted in outbursts or acting out, the best way to clear the rubbish was to give permission, give space for them to express themselves.

She looked him in the eyes, her voice emotionless and said, "Sawyer... Tell me the truth."

He was still pacing. It was as if he'd barely heard her.

"Tom," she said, louder. "Tell me the truth."

He paused, looking at her, frowning. His eyes flicked towards the guard in the doorway. "One minute!" he called.

"Sawyer," she repeated, surging to her feet. "Tell me the damn truth! Tell me! Tell me now!"

Tom just stared at her. "The truth?" he muttered. "The truth is I've gotta do this. I have to."

"Why? What did he take from you? No—not her. I know about that. I'm talking about *you.* Tell me the truth. Why?"

Sawyer let out a shaking sigh. His hands were trembling again. "You should leave, doc. Get out of here. Go to that parole hearing. Stay for a bit..."

"Coward," she said.

The moment she did, she felt as if she'd slapped him. Her eyes widened, and instantly she wanted to take it back. But then, at the way his eyes narrowed, she allowed the word to linger in all its accusatory glory.

"What did you call me?"

"Coward," she said more insistently. "You can't even tell yourself the truth. You're so scared of pain you can't tell the truth. *Coward.*"

She didn't like going this route. But gentleness wasn't received by Tom. Direct questioning was ignored. So all she had left now on a minute timer was anger. She needed his anger. But not the anger directed at her words—she needed him to tap into that part of himself that had festered. The dark, gritty, dirty, gross portion of his soul that he shared with no one else. The piece he broke parts off of at night, cajoling, coaxing, lingering, and staring.

She needed him to show it. To tell her. To show himself.

Sawyer's jaw had tightened. "Get out of here, doc. I mean it."

"Time's up!" a voice called from the door.

"A minute!" Sawyer snapped, a growl to his voice.

“We have to go!” the guard called back.

But Sawyer didn't turn. He was glaring at Ilse. “You think I'm a coward?”

She didn't say anything. The spark had ignited. His temper was burning. Now she just needed him to direct it at the proper source. The man in this prison. The one who had stolen a piece of Sawyer. A broken branch. But it could heal. She knew that much. Sometimes it didn't seem like it. Sometimes it was hard to believe. But it could heal.

“What did he steal from you?” she murmured, her voice soft again.

Sawyer was shaking his head violently.

“Tell me the truth,” she repeated, unblinking, immovable.

“Now, please!” the guard called.

“The truth is,” Sawyer muttered. “You're a damn pain in the ass, Ilse. A damn pain.” He pointed at her, grit his teeth, and then turned on his heel, declaring, “We're coming. Forget about the prisoner—I'll reschedule.”

He stalked away, without looking back.

For a moment, Ilse watched him go. But then she frowned. Not like this. She was so close. She could feel it. Sawyer was stubborn face to face. But he was also stubborn with his back turned.

But the moment he'd decided to ruin his life, he'd compromised any appropriate social boundaries there'd been. She was going to help him if it killed her.

Or him.

Dammit.

She moved around the table, half-jogging, rushing after Tom, down the long, gray hall that led back to security.

CHAPTER THIRTY FOUR

Ilse tried to catch his arm, but Tom yanked it away, still moving. She lowered her hand, walking next to him but not saying anything.

For the moment, all she wanted was to get out of this damn prison, and at least now it seemed as if this were possible. No one tried to stop them. No one intervened.

The guards by the door handed back their items. Ilse felt an urge to bite her lip. Otherwise, she wasn't sure she'd be able to hold back the words she wanted to speak.

Sawyer looked as furious as she'd ever seen him, but at least he was moving in the right direction. He jammed his keys back into his pocket on the other side of the metal detectors. Ilse followed after him, like a shadow, refusing to lose sight of him for a moment.

Sawyer didn't look in her direction.

"Hey! Stop!" a voice suddenly called after them.

Ilse froze. Sawyer turned. "Oh, thanks," he said, his voice hoarse. He accepted a couple of debit cards, slipping them into his pocket before marching towards the buzzing front door.

Ilse hastened after him, still keeping pace. No one stopped them.

Fresh air swished towards them as they emerged in the morning breeze. Ilse felt a sudden surge of relief as they left the prison, moving between metal fences and towards the gray parking lot.

"Doc, you shouldn't have come," Sawyer said, his temper still apparent.

"You shouldn't have," Ilse retorted. "Why throw everything away? You are going to ruin your life!"

They were in the parking lot now. No more guards, no more witnesses. Sawyer stood next to an unfamiliar car, his keys gripped so tightly in his hand that his knuckles were white, and a thin trail of blood spilled down his wrist from where the metal had gouged the skin.

But he didn't seem to notice. Or perhaps he wanted the pain.

Ilse tried to reach out to gently unclasp his fingers, to take the keys, but he ripped his hand away, his body as stiff as a board.

"Just leave me alone," he said, breathing heavily. "Leave. Please."

"Tom," she replied, "I'm sorry, but I'm not going to do that. I'm not going to let you back in there."

Sawyer scowled at her. "You shouldn't have shown up. Now your face is on those cameras. Did you at least use a fake name?"

She shook her head. "No, Tom."

"Christ," he muttered, turning and rubbing a hand through his hair. "It's all gone to shit. I—I was so damn close. So *damn* close."

"To what?"

He looked at her, and his eyes dropped again, but then this seemed to irritate him and so he looked up again, refusing to glance away. He held her gaze, his jaw clenched. "You know. You know why I'm here. Otherwise, you wouldn't be."

Ilse just nodded, feeling her heart rattling in her chest. She wanted to cry. Wanted to hug him. But in that moment, it was about Sawyer. About his emotions. His rage.

Anger wasn't so impressive as most seemed to think. It could scare, alarm, get the reaction that caused an endorphin rush. But anger was often a disguise for a truer, far less impressive emotion. Anger hid things. But often the only way to find what lingered beneath the anger was to remove the sediment.

"You nearly threw your life away in there," Ilse said, pointing. "I don't understand why you'd do something so selfish?"

He stared at her, still refusing to look away. "Selfish?" he murmured. "*Selfish*? Shit! I wasn't being selfish—I was looking for justice!"

"Ha! Now that's not true and you know it."

"Shut up, doc. I mean it. Shut up!"

"No. No I won't. Tom, people care about you. You can't just go do something like that without—"

"I'm nearing forty, Ilse. I'm getting a divorce. My career is spent catching monsters, but there are always a million of them. It will never end. My sister's killer..." he jammed a finger towards the prison, his voice rising in volume now, "is sitting like a giddy little puppy behind those bars. It's not right. It's not!"

"What are you saying?"

"I'm saying who the hell cares what I do with my life anyway? I need to do this, doc. I just need to. Fly to Germany. Stay away for a bit. I'll make it clear you had nothing to do with it."

"I care," she said simply.

He scowled at her. She shrugged. "I do. I care what happens to your life. That's why you're selfish. Don't you see? You can't just throw it away, Tom. Besides, you can't kill him. You know that. Don't you? It's not going to make things better. It's just going to make you a bit more like him."

"Ha! Killing a monster is not the same as killing innocents."

"No—no, I know that, Tom." Ilse stepped away from the car, giving him access towards the front door so he wouldn't feel like she was trying to trap him. But she pressed on. "It would make you a *bit* more like him. That's how these things work. Serial killers don't start as serial killers. Evil doesn't start fully made. It's the choices we decide on. Slow steps. Brief decisions. One step at a time down a path we should've avoided altogether. Sometimes you get lost. Sometimes there's no going back." She pointed at the prison. "In there... if you'd done what you wanted. There would have been *no* returning. Don't you see?"

Sawyer was shaking now, his hands trembling at his sides, his eyes still unblinking, strained.

"Damn it, doc," he said, his voice hoarse.

She repeated her request from earlier. "Tell me the truth. Tell yourself the truth."

He looked her in the eyes, inhaled, opened his mouth. Closed it again. Inhaled once more.

She didn't move. Didn't speak, just watched. Waited.

And then he screamed. Not a word. Not a sentence. But an incoherent, full-lunged bellow of sound. He just screamed at her. A gut-wrenching howl from some wounded beast. He caught himself, breathing heavily as if he'd run a race. "Sorry," he muttered. "Sorry... I—I didn't..."

"Tell me the truth," she repeated.

He dropped to his haunches, squatting in the parking lot. He clasped his head in his hands. "Doc, just let it go."

"It wasn't right what happened to you, Tom," she said softly. "It wasn't right. It wasn't fair. It shouldn't have happened. He hurt *you* too. Hurting you doesn't make him powerful. It doesn't make you weak. It just makes him evil. That's all. It's not impressive." Sawyer was still holding his head. Still trembling. Ilse kept talking, lowering next to him now, reaching an arm around his shoulders. He tensed, so she lifted her arm, but remained crouched by him. She said, "These killers want to be impressive. They're not. They're the weakest humanity has to offer. They live off other people's emotions because if they sit alone in a room with themselves all they feel is miserable."

Sawyer was breathing rapidly again. "I—I'm dizzy, doc. I don't want to think about this."

"He hurt you too, Tom. He hurt you."

Sawyer's body physically reacted to these words. Tensing again as if she'd jolted him with a taser. He screamed once more, this time at the ground as if trying to hide the sound. Again, no words, just sheer rage. An over-boiling anger and hatred. More screaming.

And then he just collapsed. Onto his knees, leaning against the car as if all his energy had left. He was sobbing now, tears streaking down his cheeks. Ugly, loud crying. Nothing Hallmark or movie credits about it. True sobbing. Real crying. Bone-deep agony spilled from Sawyer like blood.

Tears long suppressed. Tears never allowed.

He just shook and sobbed, and hiccupped and sobbed some more. Leaning against the car, his eyes closed, like a little child.

Ilse sat next to him, slowly, carefully. Not wanting to disturb him. She pressed her back to the tire. She placed a hand on his shoulder.

This time he didn't tense. He just cried. It was hard to be defensive when one was being so vulnerable simultaneously.

The two of them sat there in the prison parking lot, not speaking. Ilse sat next to Agent Sawyer, listening to him and staring off across the asphalt.

"I'm sorry," Sawyer murmured at last.

She looked at him. "Don't be sorry, Tom."

"I—I can't believe I was about to..." He bit his lip, swallowing again. "I hate him. I hate him so much. I hate..."

"I know," she patted him on the arm. "I hate sometimes too. It doesn't help, but it's not always avoidable. You don't have to feel this way, though, Tom. You don't have to."

"How?" he whispered.

She considered her own choices. Her father's upcoming parole. Her missed flight. She felt a flicker of anxiety. She felt tears in her own eyes simply out of empathy for Tom. This time she couldn't resisted leaning over and wrapping him in a hug.

He smelled of sawdust and sandalwood, even in his new suit.

"We can help each other," she murmured. "We're both going to need it."

Sawyer exhaled faintly. He swallowed. "I'm no coward, doc."

"I know that."

"I'd like to help each other. I like the sound of that." He reached up, wiping angrily at his face, muttering to himself in a sudden spurt of embarrassment. Still hugging him with one arm, Ilse reached up and gingerly took the hand he was wiping his tears away with. She held the tear-stained hand.

He didn't pull away.

CHAPTER THIRTY FIVE

Ilse sat on her bed in her apartment, nervously twisting her fingers. In the other room, she heard the TV. Also, a voice. A man's voice. She hadn't had a man over in... ever.

Just as friends, of course. Just for the company. Sawyer was watching some stupid baseball game. She didn't mind. He seemed to enjoy it and she was given the chance to enjoy the finger food he'd brought with him. Never had she seen so much taco dip.

But now, sitting in her room, she felt a surge of nerves. It was evening. The morning's events at the prison were still fresh on her mind. No calls yet from supervisors. No raids breaking down her door.

At least for the moment, Sawyer's shenanigans had been undetected.

And also, he was no longer speaking about going back and finishing the job.

"Come on, Ump! Are you blind!" Sawyer barked from the other room.

Ilse smirked, listening to the voice. She felt another jolt of anxiety that someone was in her own space. Someone she could hurt. Someone who... who needed her. And who she needed.

This wasn't a client-doctor relationship. She wasn't in control.

"Just friends..." she muttered, nodding firmly.

She glanced back at her phone, towards the text message that had chased her into the other room. She frowned at it. Part of her knew its contents before she even read it.

The unknown number had an area code from Germany. The message started: *Parole Hearing rescheduled.*

If they pushed the hearing to a later date, she'd still be able to attend.

But in her gut, she knew they hadn't. Not with him pulling the strings.

No—she didn't have to scroll down to know the contents. But she did anyway. And it was confirmed. They'd rescheduled the hearing for today—the afternoon.

She let out a shaking little breath, reading further. Like a knife between her ribs, she felt a jolt of anxiety turn to pain.

He'd been paroled.

After all these years.

Gerald Mueller was a free man.

Twenty-five years in prison. And now he was back.

How had he managed to reschedule? His accomplice? The person behind the postcards?

She just stared at her phone, her fingers limp.

Dammit.

She closed her eyes and closed her flip-phone. At least she'd made the right call back at the airport. She wouldn't have even made it in time for the parole. Then again, even if she would have, it didn't matter. Sawyer was more important.

She forced herself to smile at this thought. It didn't take much effort.

She'd never had someone who mattered more to her than her father did. Different types of mattering. For one, hatred, fear. The other?

Fondness?

Yes. She'd call it fondness. Friendship. That was it.

Besides, Ilse had considered this possibility before. Having him released wasn't the worst thing. Because now...

Her hand curled around her phone as Sawyer cheered in the other room.

She opened her eyes, glaring at the wall.

Now she could fly to Germany, using her resources to follow him. Gerald Mueller would reconnect with his female accomplice once he was released.

She'd be able to catch two birds with one stone that way.

And once she did?

Ilse let out a shaking little sigh, desperately trying not to think too long about the morning's events.

If she did, she'd cross that bridge when it came.

***

The postcard fluttered between his fingertips. He studied the glossy image. He reached for the fountain pen he liked to use. But he lowered it a second later with a sigh.

What was the damn point? They weren't working.

She wasn't *dead.*

"Why won't you just kill yourself," he muttered beneath his breath. "Just... just do what you're supposed to!"

He pushed from his seat by the window where he overlooked the lake. He wondered what Dr. Beck would think if she knew he'd been the one to purchase her old lakeside house. He giggled to himself, pressing his head against the cool glass and studying the water.

He'd done his research. My, oh my, how he'd researched.

That water, right there, was where Heidi and Hilda had battled it out. Ilse had killed her own sister in this backyard.

He shook his head, feeling a spurt of rage. He crumpled the postcard and flung it across the room.

"Dammit!" he screamed.

He got angry a lot sometimes.

But Ilse just wouldn't play by the rules. By the rules he'd set up. He'd been taunting her, sending her postcards, tchotchkes. But she was still going strong.

He'd hoped, over time, he'd be able to get her to kill herself. It had worked before. On a few others.

But Dr. Beck... she was a strong one.

He had to give her that. Or maybe just too stupid to realize when she was already dead.

He nodded to himself, standing in his shadowed bedroom.

Yes, yes that would be it. Stupid. She was very, very stupid.

He sighed, massaging the back of his hand. No lights on behind him. Even when writing the cards, he did it in the dark.

He didn't like lights. Didn't like bright spaces. He preferred seclusion, the night. He considered himself nocturnal.

Prompting her to suicide wasn't working.

Which meant he'd have to do it the hard way.

Letting her live certainly wasn't an option. Besides, he always came with a Plan B. He just never had to use it before.

He leaned over, plucking a Bowie knife off his table. The blade? No—no too easy. Too painless unless he had hours. Which he wouldn't.

A gun? Same problem. Too painless and too quick.

His mind was whirring now. He would have to think it through, very carefully. But then he'd finish what he started.

He always did.

NOW AVAILABLE FOR PRE-ORDER!

NOT LIKE NORMAL
(An Ilse Beck FBI Suspense Thriller—Book 7)

When victims of a serial killer are found with their bodies displayed in a dramatic way, FBI Special Agent Ilse Beck is summoned. Can she decode his mysterious signature and enter his mind before he claims his next victim?

In this bestselling mystery series, FBI Special Agent Ilse Beck, victim of a traumatic childhood in Germany, moved to the U.S. to become a renowned psychologist specializing in PTSD, and the world's leading expert in the unique trauma of serial-killer survivors. By studying the psychology of their survivors, Ilse has a unique and unparalleled expertise in the true psychology of serial killers. Ilse never expected, though, to become an FBI agent herself.

This killer is more deranged than Ilse could have imagined, but it's up to her to figure out what his plan is—and why.

Will she come out on top in this cat-and-mouse game, or will she fall right into the killer's trap?

A dark and suspenseful crime thriller, the bestselling ILSE BECK series is a breathtaking page-turner, an unputdownable mystery and suspense novel. A compelling and perplexing psychological thriller, rife with twists and jaw-dropping secrets, it will make you fall in love with a brilliant new female protagonist, while it keeps you shocked late into the night.

NOT LIKE NORMAL (An Ilse Beck FBI Suspense Thriller) is book #7 in a new series by bestselling mystery and suspense author Ava Strong. Future books in the series will be available soon.

Ava Strong

Bestselling author Ava Strong is author of the REMI LAURENT mystery series, comprising six books (and counting); of the ILSE BECK mystery series, comprising seven books (and counting); of the STELLA FALL psychological suspense thriller series, comprising six books (and counting); and of the DAKOTA STEELE FBI suspense thriller series, comprising three books (and counting).

An avid reader and lifelong fan of the mystery and thriller genres, Ava loves to hear from you, so please feel free to visit www.avastrongauthor.com to learn more and stay in touch.

BOOKS BY AVA STRONG

REMI LAURENT FBI SUSPENSE THRILLER
THE DEATH CODE (Book #1)
THE MURDER CODE (Book #2)
THE MALICE CODE (Book #3)
THE VENGEANCE CODE (Book #4)
THE DECEPTION CODE (Book #5)
THE SEDUCTION CODE (Book #6)

ILSE BECK FBI SUSPENSE THRILLER
NOT LIKE US (Book #1)
NOT LIKE HE SEEMED (Book #2)
NOT LIKE YESTERDAY (Book #3)
NOT LIKE THIS (Book #4)
NOT LIKE SHE THOUGHT (Book #5)
NOT LIKE BEFORE (Book #6)
NOT LIKE NORMAL (Book #7)

STELLA FALL PSYCHOLOGICAL SUSPENSE THRILLER
HIS OTHER WIFE (Book #1)
HIS OTHER LIE (Book #2)
HIS OTHER SECRET (Book #3)
HIS OTHER MISTRESS (Book #4)
HIS OTHER LIFE (Book #5)
HIS OTHER TRUTH (Book #6)

DAKOTA STEELE FBI SUSPENSE THRILLER
WITHOUT MERCY (Book #1)
WITHOUT REMORSE (Book #2)
WITHOUT A PAST (Book #3)

www.ingramcontent.com/pod-product-compliance
Lightning Source LLC
Chambersburg PA
CBHW030616310726
48979CB00003B/736

* 9 7 8 1 0 9 4 3 9 4 8 7 9 *